I0548227

Captives of Chicago

Volume 1: The Quest to Escape

"The Collapse Series"

───────────

By Lauren McKenzie

───────────

Special Request

THANK YOU FOR PURCHASING our book and supporting our Ministry. We actually have two requests – To Pray for Our Ministry and to Read this Book All the Way through. No Ministry can survive without prayers and support so we ask you to keep our ministry in your daily prayers and pray as the Lord leads.

We encourage you to Read the Book you purchased all the way through. Many Books NEVER Get Read, and the ones that do only get read the first few pages.

One of our Special Request is that if you are serious about learning the story in this book that you take time to actually read this book in its entirety – all the way through.

We all lead such busy lives nowadays and can get side tracked so easily, please take a moment to consider my words and read to the end of the book and keep us in Your Prayers.

Thank You once again for purchase. We deeply appreciate Your Prayers and Support and know that God will bless you as You continue to Bless this Ministry.

Table of Contents

Table of Content Continued . . . .

Trust in the Lord with all thine heart; and lean not
unto thine own understanding. In all thy ways
acknowledge him, and he shall direct thy paths.

Proverbs 3:5-6

Preface

===

DEAR READER,

The characters; the Hoffmanns, Tabetha Lee, and Angelica Clarke, were all birthed into my imagination by the grace of God. I must admit, this book really challenged by creativity in more ways than I would like to say, but I am extremely pleased with the finished product. This book would not be here today if it weren't for the Holy Spirit's guidance, assistance from my family, and the gracious help and wisdom of Tom Eckerd. I pray that these characters challenge you to be prepared, and give your life to Christ and pursue the Kingdom of God with amazing fervor if you haven't already. Because remember, time is always ticking away, so use your years to make a change. Special thanks also to the folks at the American Christian Defense Alliance, Inc. They were more than supportive in this writing journey! This book is part of a series called The Collapse, so be sure to watch for the next book in the series with all of your favorite characters and more!

God Bless, Lauren McKenzie.

Psalm 27:14.

Chapter One – Rock of Ages

———

"FATHER? ARE WE ALMOST there yet?" The twelve-year-old's hazel eyes sparkled with anticipation, and she fiddled with the vocabulary homeschool book on her lap.

"Yes, Suzzie. We have just entered Chicago," Fifty-year-old and former police officer and current investigative journalist Augustine Hoffmann replied.

Seated beside him was his wife, Mary Hoffmann, who was frail, motherly, and gentle. She was very supportive of her family.

"What's your sermon going to be about, Father?" Her daughter, twenty-four-year-old, homeschool graduate and EMT Elizabeth Hoffmann asked.

"The dangers we're facing today. UN peacekeepers might very well be here soon, and the murder rate is still skyrocketing," Mr. Hoffmann replied, his green eyes lighting up as usual when he talked of what he was passionate over.

"Do you think that North Korea will really give up their ballistic missile program?" Twenty-nine-year-old Sarah Hoffman, Mr. Hoffmann's daughter-in-law asked.

"Yes, I do believe so, Sarah. The powers that be don't need to bomb the land to control it, anyway," He answered.

"The globalist has wanted to take down America for a long time," Grey-eyed, and athletic thirty-two-year-old Patrick Hoffmann, a Marine on leave, and Sarah's husband added.

CAPTIVES OF CHICAGO: THE QUEST TO ESCAPE

"The people of Chicago really need to understand Scripture and be prepared," Patrick's little brother, a Corpsman also on leave, was six years younger than his older brother. Samuel Hoffmann had a reliable and witty personality, which won him lots of friends.

In the farthest seat in the Mercedes van, the youngest, five-year-old Daniel, played with Patrick and Sarah's son, eight-year-old Benjamin. They were both spunky and zestful.

The twins, eighteen year olds George and Martha, sat in front of the children and were discussing businesses they could open in their hometown of Erie, Pennsylvania.

The Hoffman's were all dressed in their Saturday's best and looked very sharp.

Even though they had been to Chicago many times before, the tall buildings still made their eyes stretch. People on the sidewalks, hurrying to and fro in a great hurry, the majority on their cell phones. Cops and busses, taxis, seemingly everywhere. It was a breeding ground for crime. And there were no trees to see the beauty of the autumn season.

After about thirty more minutes, the Hoffmanns made their way inside the church, right on time. They took a pew and quietly waited for the service to begin.

"Shall we rise and sing Rock of Ages?" The pastor's voice was calm and reassuring.

The Hoffmanns and the others rose.

"Rock of ages, cleft for me, let me hide myself in Thee...!"

After the psalm, the pastor began his sermon and told a frightening sermon about God's ever coming wrath on the people under heaven.

"A special speaker has agreed to come and share his knowledge with you all. I am pleased to introduce Mr. Augustine Hoffman," The pastor stepped away from the pulpit.

Mr. Hoffman came forward. "Hello. This town and this country is in a sad state. The things that back in the day would have been disturbing, are now perfectly acceptable. As many of you may know we are living in the last days and in the last days God makes it very clear that there will be a one world government... Jesus has told us repeatedly not to be deceived and to watch and pray.

Because our adversary the devil walks about as a roaring lion seeking who he may devour. Brothers and sisters, we have an obligation to protect our nation from the spread of globalism. The UN is nothing more than a sheep in wolf's clothing speaking peace and safety, while they plot against us. I have recently been given information that has led me to come here...to warn you that within a very short period of time-"

"BOOM!"

"Momma, look!" A young boy simultaneously pulled his mother's dress and pointed to the window.

"What?" The mother looked out the window and others did the same. She gasped. "The UN is here!" She exclaimed.

"What?!" Mrs. Hoffmann and others stood up.

Mr. Hoffmann went quickly to the parking lot and returned with gun cases and backpacks.

"James, is there a place we may change?" He asked the pastor.

"Yes, go down this hall, second door on the left," He replied.

The Hoffmanns hastily hurried down the corridor and changed one-at-a-time. When they came back, they wore tactical khaki pants, combat boots, and thin long-sleeves.

"Alright everyone," said the pastor, "Let's just wait and see what happens," he advised. They still stood up, and the adults looked grief-stricken.

The Hoffmanns wasted no time in loading their firearms.

A man with a rifle who owned a "small sporting goods shop," climbed the stairs to the roof.

UN troops had already set up checkpoints, and roadblocks, and some were even patrolling the streets.

The man raised his rifle. "YOU CAN HAVE MY GUN, WHEN YOU PRY IT FROM MY COLD, DEAD FINGERS!" He screamed, loud enough for the troops and the church members to hear. He lowered his gun.

"Oh, no, this is not good!" Susan lowered her head, despair filling her heart. The troops outside were talking on their radios, but nothing seemed to change.

Samuel peered out the window. What he saw made him freeze for a quick second. "EVERYBODY OUT!" He exclaimed. "THIS PLACE IS ABOUT TO BE BOMBED!"

The sheep fled out the front door, but the Hoffmanns, who were closet to the back door, hurried out that way, Mr. and Mrs. Hoffmann bringing up the rear.

All the Hoffmanns, except the parents, made it out before it was bombed by three grenade-launchers. The building went up in smoke and collapsed.

"Mommy!" Daniel screamed, and attempted to go back inside. Susan, who was in tears and had to strongly resist the urge to scream in terror, quickly grabbed the boy. George hastily hoisted the crying boy onto his back, and followed his siblings back to their van.

Other worshippers were in the parking lot, and UN officers took them. The Hoffmanns saw this and quickly entered their van, and Patrick who was in charge now, went around the crumbling church and drove over the sidewalk.

"There, there, don't let 'em escape!" A UN officer cried.

Was that a Russian accent? George mused.

Sounds of screams filled the van as soldiers fired with automatic firearms.

"Everyone, stay down!" Elizabeth told them.

Martha grabbed her SIG rifle and opened her door. "Martha, don't you dare!" George screamed. She ignored him. She grabbed hold of one of the handles inside the vehicle and with the other, her rifle. She shot outside killing two guards. Three took fire after her. When she ran out of ammo, she quickly ducked back in and slammed the door shut.

"Guys, we have a problem!" Patrick said loudly, but calmly, surprising himself because of how nervous he himself was.

"What is it?" George asked. He bent in the cockpit.

"A blockade!" Sarah said.

"What do we do?" Susan asked, shaking from all the adrenaline.

Martha snapped her fingers. "Brother, do you still have your Marine backpack in here?" she asked.

"Ye-es," Patrick said, not knowing what she was getting at.

"Ben, get me some grenades, you know what it looks like," she said.

"Yes, Aunt Martha," Benjamin nodded and climbed to the back. After they got closer to the blockade, the grenades finally came to Martha and George.

"It's now or never, Martha. I'll take one side and you the other," George said.

Martha nodded grimly and rolled down her window.

"On one! Three, two, one, toss!" George yelled.

As Martha threw hers she cried, "In the name of liberty and justice!" They both quickly ducked backed in, and Patrick pressed the gas peddle and they rushed through the blockade.

―――――――――

"FATHER! WE GOT COMPANY!" Benjamin yelled in his childish way.

Everyone looked in the rearview mirror. UN armored vehicles had taken up the chase. People on the streets screamed and took cover inside shops and watched the scene with horror: a van being driven crazily, dodging people and road bumps, and armored vehicles with guns on the top chasing them.

Chapter Two - Providence Provides

⸻

"HURRY, PATRICK!" ELIZABETH cried. The armored vehicles were gaining on them.

"I'm pressing the peddle as far as it will go!"

"I want my Mommy!" Daniel yelled.

Martha went over to him. "Daniel," she said firmly. "Daniel, look at me," The boy raised his head and Martha put her forefinger under his chin.

"Whining about it about it won't change anything. So stop your crying, suck it up, and start praying. And remember 'everything works together for good to those that love God,'" Martha said quickly.

Daniel swallowed and nodded, then buried his face in Elizabeth's lap.

"BANG!"

"What was that?" Sarah asked.

"They're shooting at us!" George said.

"Great!" Sarah said facetiously.

Samuel chuckled, but the tenseness of the moment didn't get away from him.

Sarah got up, picked up her rifle, opened her window, and shot out one of the tires.

"It's gonna flip!"

Patrick pressed the gas peddle, and by the grace of God, they got away just before the armored vehicle flipped, and would have hurt them. And thankfully, the flip slowed down the other armored vehicles.

Daniel and Benjamin sobbed, and so did Susan.

"Another checkpoint is coming up!" George cried. "Do we have anymore grenades?" he asked Martha.

"Five more!" She answered.

"How we looking on gas, Patrick?" Sarah asked.

"We'll get by," He answered grimly.

George and Martha did what they had just did a little while ago with the grenades.

"WE...HAVE BREAKING news. A car chase is happening currently on S State Street and the UN is in hot pursuit.

We have live video coverage we'd like to show you now," A CNN reporter said.

What they showed was the helicopter view of the Hoffmann van plowing through the streets.

"Wow!!" The reporter said in the background. "It seems as if these people have grenades! We advise everyone to stay in their homes until the UN has taken control of the situation.

"Wow! They just bombed a UN checkpoint!" The reporter cried. "The UN has offered a bounty for these enemies of the state. All we know is that they just got out of church and that this is what their transportation looks like," she said.

"THERE'S A HELICOPTER circling," Elizabeth said once she regained her composure.

"Next road...! Oh, no! They put armored vehicles there instead!" Martha yelled.

Patrick turned quickly.

"This isn't going to work, Patrick!" Susan cried. "We can't stay in here or we'll be trapped!"

"I agree," Sarah said, then turned to her husband. "What are we supposed to do? Walk to Inverness?"

Inverness was about fifty miles away, and on the outskirts of the town was the Hoffmanns 'vacation house'.

"Find me the nearest train station, Effy!" Samuel said. Elizabeth's nickname was Effy.

"Excellent idea!" Elizabeth rummaged in her purse then pulled out a map.

"Stop here! See it's right there!" She screamed.

"Once we're inside, we need to split up into different sections of the train," Patrick said as the family quickly tumbled out and grabbed their innocent looking packs.

They went under the city. When they got inside, George and Martha looked out for UN soldiers, and Patrick tried to see when the next train-.

"Everyone! Your attention please! Until the UN stabilizes the city, we will not be offering any of our services. Good day," an official looking man said.

The Hoffmanns hurried together. "What do we do now?" Elizabeth wondered.

"We steal a car," Patrick said.

Everyone gasped. "What?"

———

PATRICK WAITED FOR the UN to clear out the car dealership while his siblings took positions around the building. They had sneaked around as best as they could through the city.

Finally, the building cleared out and Elizabeth sneaked to a Fire exit.

She kicked it.

Not much movement. Another kick. More rattling. Another kick. Sarah sneaked there.

She nodded. She and Elizabeth kicked the door opened at the same time.

The door rattled opened. Apparently out of nowhere, the rest of the Hoffmanns appeared, and they entered.

Samuel had once worked at a car dealership, and he quickly decided on which vehicle to take. He settled on a Ford Transit connect that was outside the car showroom.

That would fit all of them with room 'to spare'.

"Hey, Pat! That," he pointed. Patrick nodded, and signaled for his siblings and son to put their stuff in the trunk.

Samuel rushed to where the keys would be, and looked around for the right key. Finally, after five minutes, he found it and the license plate.

He got back in a pant, threw the keys to Sarah, and they all got in.

"Desperate times call for desperate actions, all right," Benjamin said.

"What are we gonna say if a checkpoint comes up?" Sarah, who was driving, mused.

"Let's not get the cart before the horse," Patrick said.

"Okay. Well, a checkpoint *is* coming up. They sure where quick about it," Sarah said.

"Name!" The officer yelled.

"Uh... Bess Foster," Sarah said coolly.

"Why isn't there a license plate?" the officer asked.

"I purchased this only yesterday, good sir. But I can let you see it," 'Bess' replied.

"Let me see it."

"Oh...I said I can, *not*, I *will*," Sarah challenged.

The officer's jawline drooped a little bit.

"Duck!" Patrick screamed, he was in the passenger seat and had bent over so he wouldn't be seen, as the others had done.

Sarah ducked, and Patrick rose quickly and shot the officer. Sarah rose up and pressed the gas peddle. They rushed through the blockade.

Something whistled through the air.

Martha and George used their handguns to shoot outside.

Susan was looking out the back window.

"SOOVE"

"Grenade launcher!" She yelled.

The grenade hit a pick-up truck, and Patrick quickly turned off to another road.

"WHAT WE KNOW NOW, IS that the fugitives are now using a white Ford Transit Connect and that at least they are two in number. We are asking everyone that has any information to call the number ***-***-****.

There has been strong local resistance to the United Nations taking control of the city. Not only gangs, but local citizens, i.e. as in the Chicago quote, 'militia." The news reporter took a breath.

"One local even shouting from the roof of a building, 'YOU CAN HAVE MY GUN WHEN YOU TAKE IT FROM MY COLD DEAD FINGERS!' Which is a best known as a phrase from the iconic movie 'Red Dawn.'"

Chapter Three - American Modern Martyrs

A THROBBING FEELING. A stinging feeling. Mr. Hoffmann groaned; then coughed. "What happened?" He asked out-loud.

"Effy? George? Daniel?!" He cried out.

He heard a moan. "Augustine?"

"Martha? Mary?" Mr. Hoffmann now sat up. He was in a room of smoke and rubble.

"Augustine? Follow my voice!" The voice screamed.

Mr. Hoffmann got up and brushed some flecks of rock of his sweater. "Keep talking!"

"I'm over here!" Mr. Hoffmann finally found the body the voice belonged to. "Mary!" He gasped.

"Augustine!"

"Here," He offered her a hand.

"I can't, my leg's trapped!" She said in despair.

"Oh, I see it. I'll get it off in no time," And Mr. Hoffmann got busily to work. First he put his hands underneath the rock, then he lifted it up with all his might while his wife scurried out of the way.

When that was done, Mr. Hoffmann hurriedly went to his spouse's side. "Where does it hurt?"

"My leg, it feels like it's broken, dear," she replied.

Mr. Hoffman examined it. "It's thankfully not broken, but it'll hurt sorely for awhile and you'll have a great big bruise. I hope the kids got out. If they did, they would've headed to the cabin and took the car," He said.

"Right you are," Mrs. Hoffmann agreed.

"We nee-," Mr. Hoffmann was cut short because at that moment, the boys in blue helmets rushed through both doors.

"Freeze!" They screamed quickly; raising their rifles.

Mrs. Hoffmann shot a worried glance at her husband, who didn't look intimidate.

The leader did some hand gestures and some officers went to the Hoffmann parents; handcuffing them roughly.

"The woman can't walk! Her leg's broken," Mr. Hoffmann said hastily.

The leader looked unconvinced, until the soldiers forced Mrs. Hoffmann up and she fell back down as part of the act, and sort of, also, out of real pain.

The leader babbled something in Mandarin and some officers went outside and returned with a stretcher.

Mr. Hoffmann cursed softly under his breath.

The officer guarding him noticed. "You will die, American," He told him; his voice had a hint of a Russian accent to it.

Mr. Hoffmann laughed and looked the man straight in the eye. "No. And even if I die physically, my soul will forever live in Paradise. But you, Sir, if you do not repent, will burn in hell eternally," his voice was determined.

The fella looked disgusted and turned from Mr. Hoffmann.

The missus was told to sit on the stretcher and not move. After that, the procession moved to some UN armored vehicles.

Heavenly Father, Mr. Hoffmann called on Him silently. *On my own, I am weak and powerless to defend both me and Mary. Fill us with the Holy Spirit and protect us. But if we become the first American modern martyrs for You, we will go to Your home.*

Mr. Hoffmann flashed a look at his wife and held back tears. *And please protect all my children. And help us all not forsake You. I trust You. Help the people of this world. Amen.*

For some reason the words of a Christian rap song kept coming up in his head. For this reason, he unconsciously started humming the tune and rocking back and forth.

"You!" An officer said in annoyance and slight bewilderment, "Stop that!"

Mr. Hoffmann continued humming, but instead of rocking back and forth, opted to tap his foot on the floor instead. Mrs. Hoffmann must have realized the tune, because she copied him.

"WHAT *are* they doing?" The Hoffmanns were watching some boys in blue helmets nail something to a light post.

"I... Don't know," Patrick said uneasily. "I'll go out and look."

"No! I'll go," Martha objected.

"No, Aunt Martha, it's too risky," Benjamin said what they all were thinking.

"It's just as risky for anyone of us," she retorted.

"Okay. Get in and out as fast as possible!" Patrick agreed.

"Roger that, Sarge!" Martha threw over her long sleeve a casual black hoodie. She walked briskly out of the van and went to the light pole, as others were doing. She waited in queue quietly until she was able to read it.

She gasped. On the paper was written-

"ENEMIES OF THE STATE!

RADICAL RIGHT-WING CHRISTIAN EXTREMISTS HAVE HARMED A GREAT MANY UN PEACEKEEPERS.

THEIR NAMES AND PHOTOS ARE LISTED HERE.

PATRICK HOFFMANN.

SAMUEL HOFFMANN

GEORGE & MARTHA HOFFMANN

ELIZABETH HOFFMANN

DANIEL HOFFMANN

BENJAMIN HOFFMANN

SARAH LORENZI HOFFMANN

HELP CATCH THESE RADICALS BY CALLING ***-***-****.

REWARD - 10, 000 DOLLARS"

Martha walked away coolly and reported the news to her family. "So now people know our descriptions and names," She finished.

She breathed out shakily.

"Okay," Patrick said. "We need to stay focused, have faith, and be prepared for anything. Rule one - no crying. Rule two - always be vigilant. Rule three - don't voice your fears. Rule four - always be ready to fight."

He looked meaningfully at his siblings and son.

"Agreed?"

"Agreed."

"Okay. Session adjourned," He clapped his hands and went over to George. "Will you drive?"

"I'll drive," George laughed and sat in the driver's seat. "Okay! Everyone sit down and prepare for the drive," He said.

AFTER A FEW MINUTES of smooth sailing, they came close to another checkpoint. They were about to bomb it when-

"SOOVE."

"What the-," George almost cursed before he caught himself.

"George, back up!" Elizabeth exclaimed.

George pressed the reverse peddle. As they backed up, the checkpoint went up in flames.

"BOOM!"

"Go through!" Patrick screamed.

"WHAT?!?"

"GO!"

George pressed the gas peddle.

They zoomed through the flames and Elizabeth hit her head on the window.

"Effy? Are you alright?" Samuel asked.

"My head!"

"She might have whiplash, but there's nothing we can do about it know," Samuel said.

"Who did that, Pat?" Martha asked, pulling a granola bar out of her handbag.

Patrick shrugged. "The militia, I guess," He answered. "It could have been anybody," he added.

"Next checkpoint's coming up," George said.

"SOOVE"

"Not again! Brace for impact!"

The checkpoint went up in flames and they rushed through it. The only problem was, that on the other side, a gang was there.

"Patrick! What do we do?! If we continue, they'll shoot the window out and hurt someone," George said hurriedly.

Patrick let out an angry scream and at the same time stomped his foot on the floor.

"Open up in there or someone's bound to get hurt," the leader of the thugs screamed.

Patrick opened the door, he had his hand gun in his hand as he did so. When he opened the door, he shot the leader in the chest. The other thugs were shocked, giving George the ability to drive through some.

Martha covered her mouth with her palm and suppressed a scream; a man had been plowed through and shot up in the air. Her grey eyes resonated fear.

People had cleared off the streets and had taken refuge in shops or apartment buildings. As a result, the streets of Chicago were very ominous.

Susan cried and gathered the two young boys into a hug.

After a strangely peaceful fifteen minutes, Patrick jumped up with a start.

"Wheest!" He demanded. Susan was reading the Bible and George was humming. They stopped with a start.

"Zzzz. Zzzz." The hovering sound of a helicopter was growing louder every second.

"Press the darn accelerator, George!" He screamed.

George did as he was told.

Machine gun fire rained down upon them.

"Get up, chump!" Patrick took over the wheel roughly. He drove it in a zig-zag pattern.

The helicopter kept shooting, but eventually ran out of ammunition. Patrick could tell that the helicopter was still following though.

"Patrick! What is that sound?" Sarah asked.

Benjamin turned his head to the back door window. "The helicopter is crashing!" he cried.

———————————

"SKIRT! BAM!"

When the helicopter hit the ground, it went up in flames, just missing the Hoffmanns' transportation.

Everyone breathed again.

Chapter Four - "Hang Him"

MR. AND MRS. HOFFMANN were taken to a "reeducation camp" located at the Chicago Bear's Stadium (soldier's field).

Once there, Mrs. Hoffmann was taken to a white UN tent on the outskirts of the field and Mr. Hoffmann was brought to an office.

"Sir! Prisoner! May we come in?" The leader asked in Mandarin.

"Enter, Li Jie," A man inside said.

The men followed inside with Mr. Hoffmann trailing behind.

When the men walked in, a middle-aged man strangely resembling Russian dictator Stalin and a woman who looked like she belonged in a horror movie stood behind a dark wooden desk.

"Sir!" The officers saluted.

The man nodded slightly to acknowledge their show of respect and to signify their leaving.

"Ev, leave us," The man said to his wife.

"Yes, my husband," The woman with a Russian accent obeyed.

Turning his attention to Mr. Hoffmann, he asked, "Who might you be?"

Mr. Hoffmann's mind scrambled for answers. "Carl," he finally said.

The man sat down and with a fountain pen wrote something in a notebook. "And your surname?"

"Er... Gilbert."

The man again wrote on his paper. "And what is your wife's first name?"

"Uh...my wife?"

"I assume the woman that you were found with is your wife," he clarified.

"Err...uh...no. She's just some lady."

"Is that you were wearing similar clothing... Augustine Hoffmann?"

Great! he facetiously thought.

"Who are you and why did you lie? People only lie when they have a reason to," The man said, standing up and placing his calloused hands on the freshly oiled desk.

"Well... Viktor... would you tell me when you know I'm your enemy?" Mr. Hoffmann asked, taking a risk guessing his name.

The man frowned when Mr. Hoffmann called him that. He reached for his wired phone suddenly. He kept an eye on Hoffmann while he prattled in Russian.

Mr. Hoffmann had taken Russian language classes throughout high school and college, and was able to understand all of the conversation.

"How does this man know my name?!"

"Huh? He does?"

"Yes! Get me a report on this man right away! or else... Is this understood, Li Jie?"

"Yes, sir!"

Viktor put down the phone. He rummaged in a drawer before pulling out a knife. He cleared his throat. "Sir, who are you? I will only ask this once more."

Mr. Hoffmann kept a stony silence.

The man exclaimed in Russian.

Mr. Hoffmann chortled. The gentleman had called him a 'terrible goat.'

The gent looked oddly at him. "Who are you?" he asked in Russian.

"A patriot. A protector. A prayer warrior."

"Tell me where you get your source of information!" The man exclaimed.

...Silence...

"Have it your way," Viktor said. "Guards! Come in here!" Three guards entered the room. "Take this man to the dungeon. Hang him."

Mr. Hoffmann's eyes went wide when the guards nodded respectively and forced him out the room.

Hang me? Oh God...no, no, don't let it be so! He thought as the men brought him to an entrance hidden inside a janitor's supply closet.

―――――――

"YOU ARE A TOOL THAT your government uses to corrupt you. They fill your heads with corporate propaganda and get you to do their bidding for them. We need your help. Don't be a bad guy. Be a good a guy and wear a blue helmet," The TV inside the tent was saying as Mrs. Hoffmann and her guards entered.

The UN propaganda video suddenly turned into what looked liked an autumn season movie, but in reality was secretly trying to push UN agendas on people watching.

A seat was in front of the television and Mrs. Hoffmann was forced on to it.

"The socialist economy has benefitted me so much," A young woman with golden, brown hair was speaking to a man.

"Yeah, me too. I'm so grateful for the UN take over. Imagine what could have happened to our businesses if they did not."

"So true, Harold. And those psychopathic radical militia men stopped because they knew that they would never have V day."

"What is this?" Mrs. Hoffmann asked loudly.

"Quiet, matron," A UN officer hushed.

"I will not stand still for this kind of propaganda!" Mrs. Hoffmann screamed, jumping up and stomping her foot on the ground at the same time.

The UN soldiers ran to her and hit her head with the butt of their rifles. Mrs. Hoffmann slumped to the ground.

―――――――――

"CAN'T WAIT TO GET OUT of the area and near the highway," Sarah said. They had been driving for three minutes after the helicopter crash.

"Yeah," Samuel, who was driving now, agreed.

Black Antifa thugs came out of a building and stood in-front of the van holding clubs and pistols.

"Not again," Samuel moaned.

"We'll bribe 'em," Patrick says.

"With what?" Samuel and everyone asked, bewildered.

"Wraps."

Patrick rummaged into his backpack before pulling out lunch bag. "Seriously?" Elizabeth said. "Tortilla wraps?"

"Not just any tortilla wraps!" George exclaimed as he watched Patrick put a grenade in his lunch bag. "They pack quite a kick!"

Patrick sighed at the pun and in unison opened the van door. He snuck his hand into the bottom of the bag and pulled the pin before giving it to an angry look thug. With great haste, he leaped back in the van. "GO!" he screamed.

Samuel pressed the accelerator, the heat from the explosion making their getaway hot.

"Glory to the Lord!" Sarah exclaimed.

"Uh-oh!" Samuel said quietly. He was driving towards a Antifa thug who held a rocket-launcher in his hand.

Patrick groaned. "Really?!"

Patrick ran to his rifle and opened the van door. "Slingshot, Sam!" He yelled.

Samuel made a turn and, in the process, Patrick fired at the man and killed him. Once that was done, Samuel backed up and continued for their destination while Patrick closed the door.

Susan laughed and cheered. "That was epic!" She cried.

Patrick gave her a wry smile.

———————

AFTER BEING SHOVED through the opening and going down three flights of stairs, Mr. Hoffmann entered a smelly, cold dungeon area.

People of different races, religions, and cultures had their hands bound to a wooden pole hanging from the ceiling.

The guards roughly took Mr. Hoffmann to an empty spot, and bound his hands to the top of the pole.

"You will die miserably," One guard said in his face. Mr. Hoffmann kneed him in the thigh.

"Ow!" The UN officer looked at his hurt nerves: he lunged to grab Mr. Hoffmann throat.

"Bernie!" The other officers stopped him just in time.

One poured cold water over Mr. Hoffmann's head. "Enjoy yourself," he said mockingly.

Chapter Five - Yanked Back

RIGHT BEFORE THE HOFFMANN children got on the freeway, Muslims in their headdresses and long gowns with rifles stopped them temporarily from continuing their journey.

"GET OUT DE CAR!" The leader screamed. Sarah shot a worried look to her husband. "NOW!"

Patrick looked in the rearview mirror. A pickup truck was behind them. RPGs were also there.

Patrick shot a prayer up to heaven. "Slingshot," He told Samuel.

"But-?"

"Get up front," he told his siblings in the back. They did as they were told.

Patrick took out the last grenade.

"Now!" He yelled. At the same time, Patrick opened the side door and launched out a grenade, while Samuel did a slingshot again. The grenade exploded right under the pickup and tore it to pieces, while Samuel righted the vehicle and plowed through the Muslims.

To the Hoffmanns' children dismay, behind the pickup was another one that quickly took up the chase.

"What do we do?" Elizabeth asked. "We can't afford to waste any ammo."

Patrick was about to speak when an explosion happened right in front of them. "Back up, Sam, back up!" He ordered.

"Wha-?!"

"Just do it!"

Samuel looked at his other siblings. Elizabeth ran over to the cockpit and yanked back the gearstick. They sped backward and crashed into the pickup.

George ran outside with his gun, his older brothers in tow.

"You're crazy, Effy!" Susan exclaimed as the brothers outside killed the Muslims and took the guns, ammo, and RPGs.

"Hey, if Sam didn't want to do it, someone had to!" She aggressively, as her brothers came back in.

"Drive, Effy," Patrick commanded. She hopped in the driver's seat.

"These guns and ammo are all high quality," He took to his flashlight and examined a Glock 17 G 5. His eyebrows suddenly popped up as if he just noticed something.

"What is it?" Sarah asked.

"Engraved on this weapon is 'Property of the Federal Bureau of Investigation,' He answered.

Everyone gasped.

"Jus- Just great!" Sarah exclaimed angrily, voicing everyone's thoughts.

"IF ANYONE WILL TRY to rescue them, they'll get both at the price of one. Keep the matron here, move the man. Understood, Li Jie?"

"Yes, sir!"

MR. HOFFMANN WAS TAKEN from the dungeon and put in a UN armored vehicle.

"Might I ask where we're going?" he asked his guards.

They were taciturn.

"You boys can't really believe that the folks here will just let you raid their homes and take their firearms. It doesn't work that way. When you try to confiscate our firearms, believe me, you'll wish you hadn't," He said.

"Shut up!" One of the officers screamed.

"Why so defensive?" Mr. Hoffmann asked defiantly. "Or is it because you know what I'm saying is accurate?"

The officer scowled.

Mr. Hoffmann scoffed and looked away.

The drive continued and Mr. Hoffmann was brought to a local Wal-mart.

The parking lots were all empty because shipping containers and fences and armed guards filled it instead.

Mr. Hoffmann gasped when he saw it, and knew he had reached his destination.

"Get out!" The other officer exclaimed.

Mr. Hoffmann got out, and when one guard was in the process of step-ping out, he saw his chance. He yanked the rifle away from him and gained control of it.

"OW!" Mr. Hoffmann dropped to the ground.

When he woke, he was in a dimly lit shipping container whose doors where open, so sunlight shined in. He realized he was on a bottom bunk, and that other prisoners were with him. Bunks all lined the walls.

"You been out quite for awhile," A middle-aged man in a leather jacket told him.

"Have I? How long?" He asked.

"Two, three hours, at best," the man walked over and shook hands with him. "I'm Hubert Green, who are you?"

"Oh, I'm Augustine Hoffmann. Nice to meet you, Mr. Green," He responded.

"Likewise!"

"I had yanked a guard's rifle from him and somehow I fell to the ground," He said.

"Seems like you were yanked back," Mr. Green said, not quite serious, and not quite kidding.

Mr. Hoffmann gave him a wry smile.

———————

AFTER THE RUMBLE WITH the Muslims, the Hoffmann children's ride to their cabin located on the outskirts of Inverness was fairly peaceful.

The suburbs of Inverness were strongly patriotic, though were there were Liberals, they were not friendly at all.

The Hoffmann vacation cabin was located in the middle of the beautiful Illinois woodlands. The land was flat, but over the years Mr. and Mrs. Hoffmann had fortified it.

The entrance to main land was secured with a limestone retaining wall, and a very bonnie black cast iron gate.

Mind you, to get to the retaining wall, you had to drive almost a mile.

Once the gate was opened (by use of a key and padlock. If people were inside, they used a metal bar in addition to seal it off), vehicles could easily come in.

A concrete driveway under a pavilion sheltered the vehicles from rain or snow.

A slab pathway led the way to the front door.

A decent-sized white oak log cabin with a stone basement was there. You had to climb some steps to reach the front door, as the stone of the 'basement' was visible. A galvanized roof covered the front door.

Enter in and the first thing you saw was a comfortable living room with vaulted ceiling. Accent chairs, a rocking chair, and a love seat sat in front of a cozy hearth. Directly ahead was a large balcony that had a gorgeous view.

Inside to the left, an Amish wood stove with some logs in a cane basket, a cupboard filled with pots and pans, a refrigerator, another cupboard filled with packaged food, and a bread maker, summed up the total of kitchen things. An island provided eating space and cooking space.

Some stairs led up to a good-sized loft. Two cupboards of clothes, entertainment, and ammunition and firearms filled them up. There was also the only above ground bathroom. Bunks lined the wall, and two queen size beds was at the head of the banister.

Below ground, or slightly, housed more guns and ammo, and provisions and survival gear of all sorts.

PATRICK OPENED UP A box of cereal and passed it around.

"We've entered Inverness," Elizabeth declared. "'The village with a history,'" She said, quoting the town's motto.

"Great," Samuel said. It was nearing sundown. "Just head for our course."

"I hope Father and Mother are okay," Susan said.

"God holds them, and us, in the palm of His hand," Sarah said, "So we need not be afraid."

"Mmm," Susan agreed.

Fifteen minutes later Patrick was unlocking the padlock and him and Samuel were opening the gate, and Elizabeth drove the van through.

The older boys checked the house and property briefly to make sure it was free of any unwanted guest, while George stayed with his younger siblings incase there were any.

"All clear," Samuel reported to them.

"Good," Sarah said, taking her husband's offered hand for help down.

Everyone took all their gear out and put it inside.

"I'm sure I'm not the only one that's starving," Martha said as Patrick started a fire in the hearth and the rest of them took off hoodies. "Let's get some supper cooking up," She told the other girls.

"Yeah, that sounds good," Sarah and the rest agreed. They hastily went to the kitchen and Elizabeth started a fire in the wood stove.

"This house sure is cold right now," She commented.

"That's for sure," Sarah concurred as she took out carrots and onions for the chicken noodle soup they were about to make. They had already spent one night in the cabin for their visit, and had went to the grocery store.

Susan got busy peeling and cutting carrots, while Sarah peeled and chopped up onions, while Martha washed and cut up some chicken and put it to boil. And Elizabeth cleaned and cut up celery.

All of them working quickly and determinedly, the soup and some fresh baked bread was finished and plated in record time.

During that time, the boys cleaned and prepared handguns, rifles, grenades, and ammunition for battle.

"O Father in Heaven," Patrick prayed as they were all ready to eat, "We thank Thou for this food, for our refuge from people that want to harm us because we do our best to honor you, and that everything ultimately works out for our good. Keep Father and Mother safe, Amen."

As the weary Hoffmann children ate their food, everybody's thoughts were far away, on different things. But above everybody else's thoughts, Benjamin's stood out the most.

Jesus, why do you let these things happen? Why can't the world all be good? I guess I already know the answers to my questions. Jesus, please help me be like my parents and aunts and uncles. They always seem so calm, so at peace in these tough times. How do they do it, Lord? How do they trust you with everything? Help me learn to trust you with all things. Amen. Suddenly, a scripture verse came to young Benjamin's mind.

CAPTIVES OF CHICAGO: THE QUEST TO ESCAPE

The fervent prayer of a righteous man avails much.

Chapter Six - No Average Joe

AFTER THEIR EVENING meal, Patrick discussed his plans.

"You females will stay put, while me and Sam and George look for Father and Mother. We've got enough vittles to last quite a while, if need be. My guess is that they're being held at some sort of stadium.

Girls, please pack some backpacks full of ammo, grenades, and vittles. Sam, you and George ready equipment we need for our battle, while I'll set up the HAM and look for news," he said. "Agreed?"

"Agreed!" Samuel clapped his hands and the other members of the family went to do the tasks assigned to them.

Patrick set up a long-ranged ham radio. He spent quite a while flipping through channels before he found one.

"Guys, listen to this!" he beckoned to his siblings.

They came over.

"All dissents will be placed in detention camps. If you would like to visit someone you know, please call this number, ***-***-****. The United Nations had to do this because if they did not, freaks would be roaming the street, and causing chaos," came through on the radio.

"I bet that that's were our parents are!" Benjamin said.

"Most likely," Sarah said, "But it's not like we can call the number, we already destroyed our electronics," she said. During the process of escaping Chicago, the boys had destroyed all phones, iPads, and iPods.

"Besides," Patrick pointed out, "It's a trap. If anyone did call that number they could very easily be tracked."

"Yeah. So what are we gonna do, Father?" Benjamin asked.

Patrick went over to a map of the surrounding area that was next to the fireplace.

"Here's the Chicago Bears Stadium," he said, pointing to a place on the map. "After nightfall, we'll leave," He said.

It was already 5 o'clock, and it would be dark in two and a half hours or so.

"Okay," Elizabeth said, quickly taking command. "We girls need to ready your packs while you boys need to get some rest."

The boys nodded wearily and went to their bunks.

Thirty minutes later, the boys' packs were ready and the girls enjoyed some minutes of rest.

===

MR. HOFFMANN MOANED in pain.

"Who do you work for?"

....

Punch.

Mr. Hoffmann was being tortured.

===

PUNCH.

Mr. Hoffmann was in an underground shipping container; sound-proofed with carpet.

"Who trained you?"

Mr. Hoffmann tittered.

The man throwing the punches looked oddly at Mr. Hoffmann.

"Who trained me?" he tittered again.

The man went inside another room. "I don't like this man, Virgil," another man told him. "He's much too well prepared for this just to be a 'average joe police officer'."

"I think we have already established that this is no average joe, Elijah."

"Quite. Give the diktat, Virgil," Elijah said.

THE GIRLS HAD CHANGED into loose fitting jeans with sweat-pants lining, and a thyme plaid flannel shirt over top black t-shirts.

Martha climbed up the stairs to where her brothers were asleep. She went to George's bedside.

"George," she said softly, "George!"

He stirred a little bit.

"George!!"

He awoke with a start. "Martha!" he sighed. "It's only you!"

"It's time to rise, George, the moon is already up, so should you be," she responded.

"Yeah." Martha moved to wake her other brothers, and George hopped out of bed.

One by one the brothers lined up for their turn at washing at the wash-basin that their mother had picked up from a garage-sale.

After the boys had washed their face and put on their combat clothing, Sarah went outside to fill up the Nissan Titan that was Elizabeth's vehicle and that she had brought for a 'just incase scenario'.

It was a black, with sunroof and black leather seats.

After she filled it with gasoline from their stockpile, everyone filed outside.

"Let's pray before you guys go," Martha suggested.

Patrick nodded, and he began to lead them in prayer. "Heavenly Father, hear our prayer this hour. Please protect the girls and us as we do what is needed. Lord, I ask that you would help us find Father and Mother. Please, open this nation's eyes before it all collapses," he paused, fighting back tears. "If we don't come back, help them know we died fighting for freedom, fighting for You. Amen."

One after the other, the girls and little boys exchanged hugs with the older boys.

"Goodbye," Martha said to George.

"...Not a scratch, not a scratch, Patrick," Elizabeth was saying to him.

He chuckled. "Farewell, sister. I pray we shall meet again," he started the engine.

"Sayonara," she replied.

And the boys were off.

"Alright, everybody in the house," Elizabeth said, hastily taking command again.

They went back inside.

Sarah and Elizabeth went inside the kitchen, leaving Martha with the younger ones on guard.

"What are we gonna fix for a snack?" Sarah wondered.

"Hmm," Elizabeth looked inside the refrigerator. "Chocolate peanut biscuits?'

"Sounds delicious!" Sarah agreed as she went to the cupboard and pulled out a bag of flour.

"I can't wait to cut our hair," Elizabeth jested as she grabbed a Pyrex baking pan and slapped flour into it.

Sarah laughed. It had been agreed that in a grid down scenario, the girls would have to cut their beautiful long hair (because females were targeted more in a bad situation).

Susan had light brown hair that glowed in the sun. Martha a similar color, but hers was more golden. Elizabeth had the same type, however Sarah's hair was a light blonde.

———

"IS IT WORKING?"

"Yeah, thankfully it's easy to program these things," George replied from his seat in the back.

Patrick slipped an earpiece into his ear. "Never thought we would actually have to use these," he said.

Samuel scoffed. "You and me both," Samuel slipped his own earpiece in. The earpieces were connected to their HAM radios which would allow the boys to communicate to each other.

"So what's the plan?"

"Why are you asking me?" Samuel queried.

"You're the brains!"

"Since when?"

"Right now!"

Samuel sighed. They had just left Inverness and were taking a roundabout way to Chicago.

"You remember when we were young and we would explore the city by means of the tops of buildings?" Samuel asked.

"Yeah. I was just thinking that," Patrick nodded his head. "But it makes more sense use the sewers. I'll never forget when we fell into the sewers and had to find our way out."

"Huh, yeah. This is definitely going to be something I wish I never had to do," Samuel said.

"It's the price we must pay for our convictions, brother."

———

ELIZABETH BREATHED in deeply. Sarah had just washed her hair and was rubbing it dry with a towel.

Sarah picked up the hair salon scissors they had bought from Sally's. Gathering a handful of Elizabeth damp hair, she prepared to cut a foot of her hair.

"Snip, snip, snip."

Martha and Susan grinned cheekily as their sister's thin hair came to the floor. Benjamin and Daniel were eating their snacks and playing spelling games.

Thirty minutes later, Elizabeth nervously looked in the hand mirror Susan held. Her hair was now at shoulder length. Wavy curls started to appear because her hair was always curly after she washed it.

Sarah went next, Elizabeth being careful to match how good Sarah was. Sarah liked it.

Martha came, then Susan, with Sarah doing most of the cutting.

Chapter Seven - Pointed at Your Throat

———

PATRICK SLOWED HIS speed and looked suspiciously at the group of men he was approaching. They had raised their weapons, and his brothers were also prepared to open fire at the bunch. It was dark, and the city's power was being fickle.

Samuel cautiously rolled down his window, sidearm in his hand.

"Who are you?" he challenged.

The leader answered. "I ask likewise of you." the group of several bonny, hard men, wore camo pants, dark green shirts underneath a bulky bulletproof vest, and combat boots.

"Answer my question first."

"Now, you aren't in any position to be giving orders."

"A Glock 17 pointed at your throat says different."

Some of the group chuckled.

"You have wit, son" The man replied.

———

"LAST CHANCE," SAMUEL shot back.

"Alright, I'll compromise today. Former General Wesley Conner of the United States Green Berets," he answered.

Samuel shot a look at his brothers.

"Can I ask who you are?"

"Samuel Hoffmann, Corpsman for the Unites States Marines."

Conner also shot a glance at his party.

"Who's the driver?" He asked with a nod in Patrick's direction.

"My brother, Patrick Hoffmann, sergeant for the Marines, and my younger brother, George," he replied, lowering his pistol.

"Should we trust him?" George asked.

"I guess," Patrick replied, cautiously getting out of the truck.

The boys walked out of the truck and shook hands with each of the group.

"Green Beret John Prescott," a blue-eyed young man of twenty years shook hands firmly with George.

"Nice to meet you," he replied.

"Captain Fenwick Aston," A very young man of eighteen year's light grey eyes stared challengingly into Patrick's.

"We're all Green Berets, and we're proud to be. I'm Luke Macadam. My grandfather was a full Irishman," the strong forty-nine-year-old civilly shook hands with Samuel.

"Walter Gilbert. I was the sniper on our missions. John is my son," the forty something man saluted.

"Clifford Canady." a man with dark amber eyes and a mess of blond hair, who's age was about 34 firmly shook hands with Patrick.

"Amos Kimberly," Curly black hair shaped this man's face, and he was rawboned. He was only twenty-four years old.

"Pete Haskins. This is Peter Haskins Jr.," the man looked at his son of twenty-seven years who held the same characteristics as his father. Black eyes, light brown hair, and a brawny frame.

"Hi. My name is Abe," The thirty-nine-year-old man had light brown hair, light green eyes, and a firm handshake. Patrick frowned when the man left out his last name.

"What you boys doing?" General Conner asked.

"We're trying to rescue our parents from the FEMA camps," Patrick replied.

"How to you attempt to go about doing that?"

Samuel explained their plan.

"Hmm," the General said before huddling with his colleagues.

Patrick swallowed and put a hand on his CZ (type of handgun).

The General turned back to the boys. "Sons, we've agreed to help you, and burn every *single* FEMA camp along the way."

The boys' eyebrows jumped up in surprise.

The General went on. "Those...no good scoundrels burned down our church. The Church of the Trinity's building is no more."

George gasped. "The church we went to is called Church of the Trinity."

General Conner nodded. "Huh. What a coincident."

The boys nodded.

"Well. We appreciate your help. Do any of you need water or food?" Patrick said.

The group shook their heads.

"Well, gents, please come in the back of the truck," Samuel said.

The men nodded.

Some stood, and some sat down. The boys continued driving.

ELIZABETH PULLED HER now much shorter hair into a French twist and went over to the living room wash basin and started washing a dirty plate.

"Effy? Sarah? Suzzie?"

Elizabeth quickly patted her hands dry and ran to the radio. "Hello?"

"Effy! We picked up some stranglers," Samuel told her the story.

"Wow! Talk about providence!" Elizabeth said once he finished.

"Yeah. Hey I gotta go. We just reached the sewer that goes into the city."

"Alright. By-bye, Sam. God be with you."

THE MEN GOT OUT OF the truck and slipped on their packs.

"Who'll take the lead?" George asked in a hushed voice.

"I will," Abe responded.

The others assented their agreement and Abe cam in front and removed the lid. "Ugh."

Abe jumped down the hole. The Green Berets came next while the Hoffmann boys put camouflaged nets over the Titan.

"This smells so bad," John said in a low funny sounding voice.

The men continued walking.

"Sarge, where we gonna come up?" Samuel asked.

"The hole near the stadium," he responded.

"Roger."

While exploring the sewers years ago, the Hoffmann boys had sprayed glow-in-the-dark spray paint arrows on the wall as directions.

The men continued for about twenty minutes until Abe held up his fist. Everyone immediately stopped. The boys and Abe looked up.

"How are we getting up there?" John asked softly.

Abe gently slid off his pack and went into a bear-like posture. Samuel quickly caught on and stepped apprehensively onto Abe's back.

He quickly put both feet on his back. Samuel breathed out in relief that he was just tall enough to reach the top lid. Hastily but quietly he lifted the lid and slid it to the side.

Then he put both hands up top and hoisted himself up. When he got up he was face to face with a stunned UN peacekeeper. Before he was able to do anything, Samuel clicked the safety off his rifle and fired. It was almost as silent as a whisper because of the silencer. The man slumped to the ground.

Each man came up in a likewise fashion, sometimes needing help from one above.

"Now it gets fun," Samuel declared.

Chapter Eight - BOOM, BANG, BAM!

THE BOYS AND THE GREEN Berets were right next to the stadium, and the UN was obviously there. The boys decided to split up. Patrick, Abe, Clifford, and Fenwick would be in one team.

Samuel, Amos, Wesley, and Luke in another, and finally George, Pete and Peter, and John in the last.

"George, you and your team secure the perimeter. Sam, look for Mother. I'll be looking for a computer room," Patrick said, and the others agreed.

When the teams split up, George and his team went around the stadium. It wasn't long before they came across some more soldiers.

The soldiers were just as startled as their companion had been, and suffered the same fate. The men were careful to stick as close to the wall as possible so that cameras and what-not could not spot them.

THE BOYS HAD COME OUT of the sewer system right where there was a door, so while George left, Samuel and Patrick's teams stayed near the door.

Peter examined it. There were two doors, which had no knobs. He quietly reached into his pocket and pulled out a fixed blade knife. The others moved away and Peter stuck his knife in the middle, and with some difficulty, brought it to the center.

"CLICK"

The doors sprung open. Peter breathed out in satisfaction.

They entered inside. The first thing they saw was a camera.

The man watching the CCTV footage was stunned. He pushed off on his heels, and his chair went backwards. When he reached the the other side of the control room, he pressed an alarm button, then reached for a walkie-talkie.

"Intruders at door 27," he said.

"GREAT!" PATRICK SAID sarcastically as Samuel and his group split up. Patrick and his team quickly came across five UN peace-

keepers.

They quickly retreated around a corner. The bullets whizzed from both directions, and Clifford almost got hit.

"FIGHTING!" GEORGE EXCLAIMED none too quietly as they continued to circle around the stadium.

The others looked at him as if he'd gone mad.

"I have an earpiece in," George explained to them, lowering his voice. The others nodded and continued walking.

"There they are!" An officer screamed from behind a bush. The men broke up.

George continued firing. And tried to advance against the foes. He was pinned down in his spot.

MARTHA WAS PLAYING a parrot jigsaw puzzle with Benjamin before she suddenly stopped.

Benjamin, noticing his aunt's darkening face asked, "Aunt Martha? Is something wrong?"

"George is in danger," she said simply.

Benjamin gasped. Over the years, George and Martha had developed a connection that told them if the other was in danger.

Martha raised her voice. "George is in danger!"

Her sisters and brother all stopped what they were doing and walked over. No words needed to be spoken.

They all kneeled down, forming a circle, each person's hand on another's shoulder.

"Father, please protect George and all of our brothers as well as the Green Berets. God, please allow George to get out of the danger he's in. Protect us by sending Your heavenly angles to protect us. In Jesus name we pray, Amen."

———————

GEORGE CONTINUED FIRING, but his arms were going heavy; it felt as if he had been holding his rifle for hours. For some reason, the shooting suddenly stopped.

The next moment, John held up his rifle as a sign all was good. George breathed out in relief and the group continued walking.

———————

PATRICK HURRIEDLY JAMMED in another clip. The men were tiring. The officers shooting would never give up. He wanted to try something risky, but dangerous. Swallowing his fear, he screamed, a loud, blood piercing shriek.

The Green Berets looked at him, and the officers looked at each other. In that split second, Patrick killed the main officer, with the others quickly catching on. The battle ended in a matter of a few short moments.

"That was good thinking," Abe praised.

"God's thinking, Sir, not mine," he replied.

The man looked pleased at his answer and continued walking down the hall.

Not long after the battle with the other officers, a grenade rolled down the hallway. Fenwick, who was in-front, gasped, then without thinking kicked it back down.

"GRENADE!" he screamed as he ran back. They made it behind a corner and blocked their ears just in time. The whole building seemed to shake.

The roof caved in over the officers, and screams filled the ears of the men.

———

SAMUEL AND HIS GROUP had separated from his brother's group as soon as they had entered the building, and experienced their own dramas.

They had been walking for five minutes trying to find an elevator or staircase when they came across at least 10 officers.

They had tied them up and were bringing them to an elevator.

Samuel made no sign of escaping. When they were about to climb up a staircase, Samuel sneaked his hand in between his belt, and grabbed a standard handcuff key, stealthily unlocking his handcuffs.

Luke was behind him and saw. Using sign language, Luke hoped the others were watching him and said, "BP," meaning, 'be prepared'

Amos communicated this to the rest of the group.

A minute passed. They were about to walk up the staircase when...

Samuel grabbed the guard around the neck and got him in a rear naked choke, simultaneously pulling his Sig (brand of pistol) from his holster and yanking him around, while shooting three of the guards.

Meanwhile, the others had somehow managed to tackle the guards closest to them and managed to hold them down until Samuel was able to unlock their cuffs, and restrain the peacekeepers.

———————

"ARE YOU KIDDING ME?" the CCTV man banged his fist on the table. "Ho-ho! Man! These kids are crazy!" the man, whose name was Charley began speaking into his radio.

———————

GEORGE AND HIS GROUP had already covered most of the first side, and were about to continue when they were faced with a very large tank.

John said what they all were thinking. "That's big."

The others nodded and they continued.

Old Mr. Pete seemed to notice something from the tank. He held up his fist.

"GET BACK! THE THING'S READY TO FIRE!"

"BANG!"

As George his group were running to a sewer drain, the cartridge went off and landed about 90 feet from them. They made it in the sewer system just in time. When they entered, they ran as far away as possible.

PATRICK AND THE OTHERS breathed out in relief when George's drama reached their ears, Patrick telling the others what was happening.

"Thank you, God," Clifford breathed.

They took a couple minutes to recover. Meanwhile, Charley fainted at his desk.

"Let's go," said Abe, getting up and walking down the hallway while the others followed.

SAM AND HIS GROUP HAD recovered their weapons when Luke came over to them after searching one of the men's' clothes.

He was holding a slip of paper. He opened it up and gasped. "This is a layout of the building's rooms!" he exclaimed.

The others gasped and hurried over to him.

"Amos, search the others bodies, won't you?" Luke asked.

Minutes later he came back with another slip of paper.

Samuel held his PTT button as he studied the paper.

"Patrick, come in, over," he said.

"Yeah, what's up? You found something?"

"Yeah..." he passed as he looked for door 27. "Where are you?"

—————————

PATRICK LOOKED AROUND for a landmark. He spotted a janitor's supply closet.

"Uh...janitor's supply closet 17?"

"Good!" Samuel sounded excited. "Keep walking then at the next left turn, take the hallway down. At the end you'll come to a staircase. Walk up it for 4 flights. When you reach floor 4, walk down the large hallway until you come to the end of the hall with a door labeled, 'Security Control Center.'"

"How do you know all this?!" Patrick cried.

"That's for me to know and you to find out..."

Chapter Nine – Unwanted Guests

SARAH SHOOK ELIZABETH vigorously. The sensors under the driveway had just went off.

Elizabeth gasped when she awoke. "What's going on?"

"We seem to be having unwanted guests," she declared.

Elizabeth gasped again then hopped out of bed and pulled on her shoes. Her hair was already tied back, and the last thing she had to do was through over her undershirt a sweater.

She and Elizabeth went to the gate with Martha guarding the younger ones inside. Sarah and Elizabeth climbed up the rough wooden ladder against the wall and climbed on the balcony like structure, ARs ready to rock and roll.

A JEEP rolled down the driveway with headlights on. Sarah frowned and looked at Elizabeth. Elizabeth also looked perplexed.

"Who are you?" they hollered from their perch.

The driver rolled down the window. "Dakota and Nellie McFarlane," the voice said.

The girls gasped. Their neighbors from home!

Elizabeth said, "What's the name of our dogs?"

"Winter, Teddy, Jordan (female)," a female voice said.

"What are their breeds?" Sarah queried.

"King Shepherd, Akita, Australian Shepherd," the female voice said again.

Before Sarah could object, Elizabeth climbed down and unlocked the gate. The JEEP rolled in.

The doors immediately opened and two bodies tumbled out.

Siblings Dakota and Nellie hugged the girls and then wordlessly went to the back and opened the hatch.

Three fury friends tumbled out. Elizabeth gasped, dropped her rifle and hurried to her dogs.

"What are you doing here?" Sarah asked as Elizabeth clipped tether on the dogs.

When the teens remained silent, Elizabeth said, "We should go inside," they nodded and followed her inside.

When they got in, Martha's rifle rested on the loft rails, looking down their throats. She looked surprised.

"Nell! Dak?" she moved her rifle and put it on safety then grabbed the rope hanging from one of the rafters that Patrick had installed for fun. She climbed down the rope easily and then hurried over to her best friend, Nellie.

Dakota and his older sister looked traumatized. Elizabeth noticed this, and also noticed her younger siblings staring at the scene with wide eyes. She beckoned for them to come down. Susan and Benjamin did so using the rope, but little Daniel chose the stairs as he was still learning how to use the rope.

"You want us?" Susan asked when they reached Elizabeth.

"Yes. Suzzie, whip up a quick meal that's hot. Boys, get extra clothes and warm blankets for Dak and Nell," she told them. They all nodded and ran off.

As she set her AR-15 against a wall, Sarah led the McFarlanes to the sofa.

They sat down gratefully. Nellie's face was a pale white, and her brother's was not much better. Her gray eyes that most times shined looked tired. The Hoffmann girls sat in one of the armchairs as Dakota prepared to speak.

"Your-..." he took a deep breath. "Your home is burnt to the ground."

Tears sprang to Elizabeth's eyes, and Sarah's too.

Elizabeth cleared her throat. "What happened?"

"UN Peacekeepers came to the neighborhood," said Nellie, "and kicked in your door. They had quite a time kicking it in," here she gave a bitter laugh. "By the time they had done that, a crowd had formed. Our parents watched in silence and finally when they dragged out your guns... *all* of them. Our parents decided to intervene, and the next thing we see is guns looking down their throat. My dad tried to escape, but it was futile. They shot him, and..." Nellie swallowed. "And they also shot my mom."

Dakota picked up the story. "We ran inside, grabbed some dog leashes for your dogs we were watching, then rushed to some empty backpacks and filled them up as fast as we could with food, clothes, and sentimental items. Then we rushed to the backyard and got into the JEEP. The UN put up a chase, but thankfully lost us on a backcountry road. We came here because we knew you'd be here."

Sarah shot Elizabeth a glance that said, "They should have listened."

Elizabeth nodded.

SUSAN RUSHED TO THE fridge and pulled out some organic hot-dogs, farm fresh potatoes, and eggs.

Grabbing the cast iron skillet from the top of the stove and adding wood to the stove, she put butter in it, making it sizzle. Then she added in the hotdogs and put on the lid. Then she turned her attention to the potatoes, she washed them really well, then put them in a cast iron pot with water in it. After they had boiled, she cut them up then put the potatoes and scrambled eggs in it.

MEANWHILE, THE LITTLE boys went up the loft to the cup-boards. First, Benjamin got blankets, then Daniel got out clothes for the McFarlane siblings.

Daniel walked over to Benjamin with the clothes he picked out. Ben-jamin raised his eyebrows when he saw his young uncle's clothes for Nellie. It was a long, breezy summer dress.

Benjamin took it from him and walked back to the cupboard, put it up and took out jeans and a long sleeve top.

"This is much more practical, Dan," he told the smaller boy.

Daniel's lip went it a pout and he stomped off.

Benjamin laughed then went down the stairs to give the blankets and clothes to Dakota and Nellie.

BEFORE PATRICK AND his team made it fully to the control room, they ran across a secretary and janitor. The secretary was armed with a handgun, but was no much for the group's automatic weapons.

When they finally reached the control room, Patrick knocked softly at the door, though a camera was right above. Hearing not even a single hushed word, Clifford motioned for Fenwick to come near with his lock picking kit. Fenwick picked that lock in record time.

Using the butt of his rifle to push it open, Patrick opened the door while the Green Berets rushed inside.

All they saw when they got inside was a fainted IT.

"Just our luck!" exclaimed Clifford as he grabbed a bandana from his pocket and simultaneously with the other hand grabbed handcuffs.

Abe and Patrick picked up the man when he was gagged and tied up to a corner in the room.

"We're in," Patrick said to his brothers over the comms line.

GEORGE AND HIS TEAM were just approaching the main stadium entrance when he heard Patrick's message.

"They found the control room!" he declared in a whispered shout.

"Great!" the others responded.

When they took positions near the heavily guarded entrance they saw an American Military Tank.

"Hopefully it's not manned," said John to George.

George gave him a "that's not funny" look and rolled his eyes.

―――――――

SAMUEL AND HIS TEAM took the stairs to the highest level possible and ran into only a group of three guards.

They, like their unfortunate compatriots, met the same fate.

When they finally saw the stadium from above, their mouths dropped open. Everywhere people were, on the seats not too far up, in tents on the field itself, and of course, *lots* of UN troops. Lights streamed everywhere, but the darkness helped somewhat.

Samuel reached into one of his backpack pockets and pulled out a polaroid camera. He took a shot then handed it to Amos. Amos shot *him* a bewildered glance then put the photograph into his pocket.

Samuel did some motions with his hands and the others seemed to know what to do since they split up and used the chairs and other things to hide themselves.

Samuel took a pebble out of his pocket and moved behind cover. He flicked the pebble towards a guard. Out of job duty, the officer moved towards Samuel's place of cover. He bent down with his back facing Samuel and examined the pebble.

Samuel leapt out and dragged the guard back with his favorite move, a rear-naked choke and pounded his head once with the butt of his rifle.

―――――――

GEORGE AND JOHN SNUCK around the tank while the son and dad group did the same on the other side.

There were no UN guards, only cameras. And George and his group figured that the UN didn't expect anyone to be able to get *this* far.

Chapter Ten - That Was Easy

LUKE HAD JUST FINISHED off a guard when a dissent noticed him very briefly. The young girl quickly looked around to see if anyone else had saw. They hadn't. Her Titian hair looked grimy and her hiking boots felt worn. She tossed off her blanket and started to stretch, and of course, a UN officer looked at her sternly, but held his peace.

She decided to do something risky when she noticed movement in higher seats above her. She pulled out her hair clip and held it snuggly in her hand.

"Sir," she said addressing the guard. "Do we get to take showers?" He looked at her and scoffed.

She plunged forward, tackling the guy and using her hairpin to dig in his eye. He was about to scream when a bullet whizzed and hit the officer in the throat. The girl gasped and got up, dragging the dead man behind some seats and taking his weapons. She was surprised no-one had seen. And terrified to see someone die. She met Luke on his crawling way.

"Who are you?" he asked in his slight Irish brogue.

"My name's Tabetha Lee and I helped organize Chicago Underground." Luke's jaw dropped. The young, innocent girl didn't look suspicious at all.

He finally replied. "Your uncle founded that in 2001! I'm part of it!" Chicago Underground was a secretive organization that very few were allowed to be apart of, and to get in you had to have connections and undergo severe vetting. It consisted of police officers, retired Army folk, Christian Preppers, and people like doctors, herbalists, and engineers.

"That's right. At church he went off the deep end and shouted "You can have my gun when you pry it from my cold dead hands."

Luke gaped again. "I was at that service! And so were the others!" he said in a shout whisper.

"Really? What a coincidence. Well, I wasn't there because I was trying to follow up on a hint that this would happen today."

"Guys?" Samuel almost got shot by the two. "What are you doing? Now's not the time chat."

He suddenly caught the face of the girl, and raised his rifle in surprise.

"It's fine!" Luke exclaimed in haste. "She's with us. Her uncle founded Chicago Underground."

Samuel looked surprised still. "Well get going, we ain't got all day!"

"Wait!" shouted Tabetha as quietly as possible. "A surprise attack would be better. I know a good portion of the people down there, and they will help when the time comes. If you try to finish the soldiers off one at a time, they'll catch on! Position your people near the main guards and the machine gun in the middle of the field on the platform. Take them out simultaneously."

Samuel and Luke quickly agreed, and met up with the others.

"CHARLEY! OPEN THE DARN door!" Patrick and the others rushed for their guns, and Fenwick placed himself about five feet from the door while Clifford opened it.

Fenwick shot the man in front, and the others finished off the rest from the side. One problem though...people in other rooms on the same floor noticed, and came out with their guns drawn.

Clifford slammed the door shut just as Abe rolled a grenade out the door.

"Bang!"

"Well, that was easy," Fenwick said dryly.

"Sam? George?" Patrick talked into his microphone. "How's it going? ... What? Really? Okay. We need to hurry this up."

=========

"READY."

"Now."

George and his team rolled a grenade through the stadium doors.

"BANG!"

"???!" - Hand grenade!" someone shouted.

There was no firefight. The soldiers inside had been bombed. George and his team went inside.

=========

"GEORGE?!" SAMUEL SPOKE hurriedly. "Get your team over here!" Patrick, we need you to split up. Leave Clifford in the security room and get over here!"

It was at least thirty minutes later when they all showed up. "What took so long?!?" exclaimed Samuel when he saw them. Tabetha had observed that the soldiers were attempting to be more vigilant, and there was more movement in the camp.

Finally, everyone was in their designed locations. "Now."

Fenwick and Abe quickly took out the surprised guards of the machine gun while Tabetha, Luke, and Samuel fought for the bigger gun. The rest of the gang fought in different sections of the stadium. When Samuel and his group gained control of the machine gun, and the dissents scattered, he shouted with a megaphone he had found, "Mr. and Mrs. Augustine Hoffmann!"

―――――――

MRS. HOFFMANN CLEARLY heard the call from her son. All of her guards had rushed to the fight, but she was handcuffed, as with others, to her chair. They were very hard silver chairs, and both of her hands were bound. She gasped as a bullet rushed through the tent material and out the other side.

Lord, help me, she thought.

She then remembered she had a bobby pin in her hair. She bent her head down as moved it toward her hand. With some difficulty, she finally grasped the hair pin. With it in her hand, she separated the two pieces of wire with her thumb and managed to straighten it in to a wide V shape. Then she had no difficulty in escaping the cuffs. Then she quickly worked on her other hand, being much quicker since she was free from one bond.

Finally, she escaped both cuffs and hastily and cautiously left the tent. A heated firefight was going on between the disgruntled UN officers, dissidents, and of course the Hoffmann boys and Green Berets. It took a moment for it to all sink in.

Mrs. Hoffmann looked around for a weapon. She spotted a Sig next to a water bucket. She grabbed it and began fighting and looking for her boys all at the same time. She spotted some militants from atop a machine gun post, and it was obvious who they were fighting against.

She ran to it and was astonished to be face-to-face with her son Samuel. "Sam!" she screamed and they hugged.

"Mother!" said Samuel after they hugged, "Get outta here! Use the sewers!"

"May the Lord protect you and your brothers!" she said as she ran to the stadium exit.

JOHN SAW THIS AND RAN to her. "Ma'am, follow me! This way will be targeted more than a normal door!" Mrs. Hoffmann quickly agreed, as she could see he was a Green Beret.

John took her through the offices and out door 27 as fast as possible. All this time, Mrs. Hoffmann had no time to think of her husband until she was alone in the sewer. During the time she traveled with John, Clifford had rushed to the battle.

"BROTHERS? MOTHER'S alive!" Samuel told them through the coms line.

"Yes!" exclaimed. "George?"

"I heard!" he replied excitedly. "Praise Jesus!"

"John's taking her to the back-way passage," he told George.

Silence.

Patrick began to feel nervous after his brother didn't respond for another minute. "Why didn't George respond?" he heard Samuel say as he and his group charged a circle of troops.

"YOU MOVE AND I BLEW you to pieces," a voice with a hint of a Chinese accent told George as he ran around a corner. George froze in his tracks.

"Lower gun!" the man told him. George released his gun.

"Psst," came from behind the man. The man looked behind him and George knocked him across the jaw with a right-hook. George recovered his rifle and looked around for where the "Psst" came from. He couldn't find it.

He was confused. Surely the voice came from someone. It was as if time had stood still.

"George!" a booming voice from the side snapped him out of his thoughts. It was Abe.

Then he remembered that his brothers had talked about him just before he was momentarily captured. "Guys? I'm alright. Got held up for a minute, that's all."

"Good!" came Samuel's voice.

Patrick then said, "Let's get gotta here! The people are fighting their battle. We've done our duty. Let's clear out!"

Chapter Eleven - Bruised and Battered

"WE DIDN'T EVEN THINK of that!" Patrick raged. "Blasted!"

"And we didn't get a chance to thank Tabetha for all she did," said Luke.

They were walking in the sewers back to the truck, and Mrs. Hoffmann had told them about how Mr. Hoffmann wasn't there.

"Tabetha?" asked Mrs. Hoffmann.

"Tabetha Lee," explained Samuel. "She's helped organize-"

"Chicago Underground," Mrs. Hoffmann finished.

"Uh-huh."

"The girls, how are the girls?"

"The girls!" exclaimed George, hurrying to make contact with them.

"THIS IS GOOD, SUZZIE," complimented Nellie quietly as she ate what Susan had prepared.

"Thank you," she replied as she poured some milk into Benjamin's cup from her special white stainless steel pitcher.

"It appears that you and your family were right about doomsday," Dakota said reluctantly.

"It isn't doomsday yet, but it could very well be soon," Martha said. They had already explained the events of the day.

Long conversations by the fireside with Mr. and Mrs. McFarlane between the older Hoffmanns and the McFarlane parents had often been discussed. They talked about things like the Mandela Effect, Time Travel, the rapture, and politics. But they never listened. The Hoffmanns felt that the McFarlane's hearts had been compelled on some occasions, though.

But they had never made a change.

Static.

Elizabeth was immediately alert and went over to the radio.

"Girls?"

"Mother!" Sarah and the others rushed to the radio. Everyone began talking at once.

"Are you alright?"

"What happen?"

"Is Father with you?"

"Quiet, quiet, everybody quiet!" screamed Elizabeth. "Mother, is everyone okay?"

"Elizabeth! Yes, everyone's fine. Bruised and battered, and shaky, but alive and breathing. No one got shot. How is everyone there?"

"Fine, Mother. How's Father?"

......

"Mama?"

"Your father's not with us, darling."

"What? What happened?"

"We were separated when taken to the stadium."

"What are you going to do?" Sarah asked.

"Come back there and regroup," Mrs. Hoffmann replied.

"Nell and Dak are here," Susan told her.

Mrs. Hoffmann gasped. "Why?"

Everyone shot Susan a look. "We'll tell you when you get here," responded Susan. "Don't worry about a thing. We love you."

"I love you girls, too."

———————

"MAN, YOU LOOK HORRIBLE," Mr. Green told Mr. Hoffmann when he finally returned in the shipping container.

"Thanks for that," he said weakly as he slumped on his bunk. He fell asleep, exhausted, and woke up when Mr. Green poured water on his head.

"What was that for, Green?" he asked in annoyance.

He nodded in the direction of the shipping container entrance. An old woman passed out bottles of water and hot sandwiches to the people inside, then left. "What is this?"

asked Mr. Hoffmann.

"What's look like? Supper," replied Mr. Green.

"Supper?" Mr. Hoffmann sat across from Mr. Green and conversed about random things: politics, the UN, movies, and religion.

"I just wanna get home to my family. I only had my hands to protect them. But if I get my hands on guns, again..." Mr. Green smirked.

"You'll get out," Mr. Hoffmann said.

"How can you be so sure?"

"My kids will come for me," Mr. Hoffmann replied.

Mr. Green scoffed. "Yeah. You said it yourself. *Kids.* What are they going to be able to do against an army of well-trained soldiers?"

Mr. Hoffmann's face turned red with anger and he got up and laid back down on his back.

My faith is in God, He controls my children, and what happens to us, Mr. Hoffmann thought. "*The Lord thy God in the midst of thee is mighty; he will save, he will rejoice over thee with joy; he will rest in his love, he will joy over thee with singing.*"

"OH, IT FEELS SO NICE to sit down in safety!" exclaimed Mrs. Hoffmann when she sat down in the truck.

"I'm sure," George said. "I hope we don't look so conspicuous riding through Inverness," he said thoughtfully.

Patrick chuckled. "Maybe...or maybe not."

"Did they do anything to you, Mother?" asked Samuel.

"Well, I think they hit me on the head. It hurts. But I'll be fine. They also tried to pour propaganda into my head, but I literally couldn't sit still for it and that's why they hit me," she answered. "How did you get out of the city?"

"Eh..." Patrick hesitated.

"Patrick..." Mrs. Hoffmann said in a mother tone.

"Well..." so Patrick told her about all the car chases, explosions, and blockades they had to deal with. Of course, she gasped ever so often and Samuel and George added their perspective of the story and sound effects.

"And how did Nellie and Dakota end up here?" she queried.

"They are?!" the boys said in unison.

"You didn't know?" Mrs. Hoffmann said in surprise. "Well then, it must have happened when you left! Something *must* be wrong!"

"I hope not," Samuel stated.

———————

"WE HAVE SOME TROUBLING news to share with our friends in Chicago...in the midst of their trouble, a California state official has just leaked California's plan to break away from the United States of America!"

Susan gasped and ran down the stairs; she had been trying to fall back asleep, and hoped the radio would hum her back to her dreams.

"Effy, Sarah, Martha," she screamed as she slid down the rope.

The older girls' eyes looked heavy as they addressed her. "Calm down, Suzzie, deep breaths," instructed Martha.

"Cal exit is really happening! I heard on the radio that they're beginning the process!" she told them.

The older girls looked at each other.

"HUSH, EVERYONE!" GEORGE exclaimed suddenly. "I think heard some static through the comms line!" they all hushed.

"Boys?"

"Martha??"

"George! California is going to move away from the Union! It was leaked!"

"What?!?" all the boys said at once.

"Yes! I don't know any more. God protect you!" Martha disconnected.

"That's crazy!" Samuel exclaimed.

"For sure," Patrick concurred. "I wonder what will happen next?" he said thoughtfully.

"Hmm. What a second, here, what time is it?!"

Patrick looked at his tritium military watch, "About 2 o'clock," he replied.

George did some quick calculations in his head. "That's 11 o'clock in Cali! Why would the leaker say something now?" he cried.

"Maybe he didn't have a choice," Samuel said.

"You're probably right. Maybe people tried to kill him!"

Oh boy, thought Patrick.

Samuel saw Patrick's ashen face and looked at him curiously, but didn't say a word.

"There's lots of possibilities for what could happen," Mrs. Hoffmann said. "EMP, China invading, Muslim sleeper cells activating," she sighed. "I hope Augustine is alright," she commented.

George patted her hand. "All we can do is pray," he said comfortingly.

Samuel raised his eyebrows as they turned onto the main road. A light fog was coming up. In the early morning hours, plus the cool breeze, and the fog, made things seem very eerie. And they all voiced that by *not* speaking.

"Creepy." George said after awhile.

<hr>

SARAH SPOTTED THAT Benjamin's eyes were rolling behind the back of his head. "Alright. Let's say we go to our bunks, eh? We'll need every bit of rest bit of rest we can get since the boys are going to be here soon. I'll wait for them." They others nodded and went off.

<hr>

"HOW MUCH DO YOU WANT?"

"How much are you offering us?" a man and women who both had evil manners were talking with as high ranking UN officer.

"$6,000 for both of you. No more. Do we or don't we have a deal?" The man looked Chinese, but had a perfect American accent.

The man and woman looked at each other. "$7,000. No less," said the woman. She had unnatural dark red hair, a fat body, and piercing eyes. The man was raw-boned, and had the same demeanor as the woman.

"No," the officer said firmly. "If you don't want the money, so be it," he paused. "Last chance."

"$6, 050," the woman said.

The two people shook hands civilly with the officer.

"We want information about these people. Their mannerisms, location, hobbies, relatives, et cetera. And you better not make this stuff up," he said threateningly.

"We'll be doing our own research. Searching the city archives," the man said.

"We're the best at what we do, Jing, we'll get your information," said the man.

"Do we have a time limit?" the woman asked.

"Seventy-two hours. If we hear nothing by then, no more money," the man slapped in her hand 2,000 dollars in advance then walked away without a word.

"Let's get started, Delilah, we haven't a moment to waste," the man told her.

"Indeed that is true.

Chapter Twelve - Can and Will

———

"PATRICK! MOTHER!" SARAH rushed out to meet the newcomers.

"Sarah!" Patrick and Mrs. Hoffmann gave her a hug.

"How is everyone?" Patrick asked her.

"Oh, the others are sleeping. Uh...we heard some news from Dak and Nell." They stopped walking at her tone, the Green Berets even though they were quite clueless, remained silently respectful.

"What is it?" Mrs. Hoffmann asked.

"The house is burned to the ground," she said bravely.

"Anything else?" Patrick asked dryly, and put his head down as they resumed walking.

"Yes," Patrick's head jerked up in surprise. "Dak and Nell's parents have left this world."

Mrs. Hoffmann gasped and searched Sarah's face for more information.

"Let's go inside," she said. Then she realized more than three people around.

"Who are they?!" she cried.

"Woah! Calm down, Sarah," Samuel said hastily. "These are our friends, the Green Berets," he explained.

"Oh, I forgot. Effy told us already."

"We're part of the local militia, too," Luke added.

They entered the cabin.

"This is real cozy," Wesley said.

"It's *really cozy*, sir," Mrs. Hoffmann corrected. She had been an English Grammar teacher in her early years, but then she got married.

The other Green Berets chuckled and General Conner swallowed uncomfortably. "Uh...yes, ma'am."

"Mary Hoffmann," she said. "And you would be?"

"General Wesley Conner."

"Make yourselves comfortable, gentleman," Sarah said. "I'll get some cool apple cider."

"Thank you, ma'am," Luke said politely.

"George!" Martha said from the loft, then slid down the rope and gave him a hug. "Brother, you were in danger, what happened?" she asked with concern.

"Martha...it's been a long night," he said with a grin.

Martha looked surprised then said with understanding, "Of course, I understand. I'll help Sarah." She looked at all the tired men in the living room. *She'll need the help*, she thought as she walked in the kitchen.

"Oh, Martha," Sarah said when she saw her. "I'm glad you're here. Make a big pot of grits, won't you?" she went out of the kitten with a tray of cups and nibbles.

"Alright," Martha responded. The Hoffmanns absolutely *loved* grits and eggs for any meal.

She got out a big pot and added a lot of water, then she added lots of salt, butter, and a pinch of sugar. She then went back into the living room.

"I had heard the drive alarms go off, so I went to wake Effy. And we left Martha in charge in here," Sarah looked at her as she sat on the floor. She then told the story of how Dakota and Nellie's parents were killed.

Mrs. Hoffmann's eyes went up in tears when she heard about the burning of her house. "Please excuse me," she said and ran into the kitchen.

Martha shot a glance into the kitchen.

"Martha," Mrs. Hoffmann called, "Your water's boiling."

"Oh," she went into the kitchen.

"Mama, are you alright?" She asked as she added in the grits.

She sighed deeply. "Sometimes I have trouble believing...that all works out."

"Mama! Come on," Martha stirred her pot like crazy.

"If Juliana von Stolberg [helped the Netherlands gain independence from Spain] kept her faith after losing *four* of her *five* sons, *selling* her family treasures, and raising *seventeen* children, don't you think you can keep your faith, having all of your children *alive* and well?"

Mrs. Hoffmann smiled and dried her eyes and looked proudly at her daughter. "Yes, I can and I will," she looked at her daughter stirring the pot. "Let me do that," she said.

"Are you sure?"

"Yes."

===

"SO, YOU HAVE NO IDEA where your father is?" General Conner was asking Patrick when Martha came in the room.

"That's about right," he replied.

Sarah sighed heavily. "What's the game plan, Patrick?" she asked.

"Revamp. Physically, emotionally, and mentally. "

The others nodded in agreement.

"No, no, no, I mean, in *general*, what's our plan?"

"Oh. I don't know. Any suggestions?"

"Well, since we can't know for certain where exactly Father is, why don't you raid all the FEMA camps you come across?" Martha asked.

"That is...a possibility," Patrick replied slowly. "But that'll take time. We're in danger as long as we stay here."

"Ye-es, but Father's worth that time," Samuel said.

Patrick sighed deeply. "Yeah, but I don't really feel comfortable having the women and children here since the UN will frantically be searching even harder for us," he explained.

"Excuse me?" Sarah said high-strongly. "You, sir, I believe, you under-estimate the women in this family. Besides, there *is* a male here, if that's what you're concerned about."

Patrick scoffed and rolled his eyes. "I never said you couldn't make out alright...but..."

"It is the Lord Who defends and protects us. Not man, weapon, or artillery," Martha retorted, helping Sarah's case.

Patrick was about to open his mouth to speak, but Martha wasn't through. "'I will lift up mine eyes unto the hills, from whence cometh my help. My help cometh from the Lord, who made heaven and earth.' See? You have no excuses, brother," she finished.

The Green Berets shot each other looks that said, "This family is very... *interesting.*"

After a couple awkward seconds floated by, George asked Patrick, "Well?"

"Alright. Point very well taken. We'll destroy every FEMA camp until we find Father," he turned his attention to the Green Berets. "Will you be leaving, or assisting?"

The men shot each other looks. "Assisting," General Conner simultaneously lifted his eyebrows in a devilish way. He then caught sight of Winter, the Akita. George must have noticed too, because he jumped up and petted him. "That's one huge dog," he commented.

"Sarah!" Mrs. Hoffmann called from the kitchen, "help me plate!"

"Excuse me," she said, picking up the empty nibbles tray, which had hastily been cleared.

"You men must be very tired," Martha said, "I'll get bedding supplies," she was about to get up, but John's voice interrupted.

"Oh, no thank you, Miss, we have blankets and all," he said.

"That's good," she replied, and rested back down.

———

MRS. HOFFMANN WAS BRINGING down lots of bowls from the cupboard when Sarah came in.

Sarah hurriedly put the tray on the island and took the bowls from her.

"Oh, thank you, dear," Mrs. Hoffmann said gratefully.

After the two plated for awhile, Mrs. Hoffmann said, "Make sure you and the girls keep up Sue and the boys' schooling. They'll need everything they can digest before everything just completely goes to rot."

"That's a good idea. Thank God that we brought their books," she said.

Mrs. Hoffmann nodded as they walked out of the kitchen.

The children had not been educated 'normally'. Instead, Mr. and Mrs. Hoffmann developed their own curriculum using 19 century schoolbooks, and the children enjoyed it. Elizabeth had got her EMT degrees almost easily, and Martha had passed her GED with flying colors.

And the children were fluent in German, plus Elizabeth was very curious about codes, and breaking them, especially the Bible Code. So, she learned Biblical Hebrew, and was in the processing of training in IT work before Chicago fell.

And of course, Mrs. Hoffmann being an English teacher and all, the children had no issue with grammar.

Martha enjoyed bush craft and photography work. She flocked with George to many historic sites and took photos of them, and put them in scrapbook albums with the history of the site attached.

Sarah loved learning about healing properties of plants, as a profession, taught her wisdom to people.

Susan loved arts and crafts. Knitting, sewing, drawing and painting, plus she was a huge organizational and cleaning freak, but it was in Hoffmann blood. All the Hoffmann children grew to love cleaning, organizing, and decorating their rooms.

Money each month was a joint effort. Mr. Hoffmann was a private de-
tective, Mrs. Hoffmann wrote encouraging Christian Books, Patrick
and Samuel were in the Marines, Sarah had her classes (which were a
little pricey!), Elizabeth was an EMT, and Martha worked at the grocery store, also Elizabeth designed websites and Martha sold her photographs, and George was an outdoor wilderness guide.

All in all, the Hoffmanns were pretty wealthy, and had the largest house
in the neighborhood.

———————————

THE HEAVY DOORS WERE pulled back, waking Mr. Hoffmann
and the others. Several troops came and roughly took Mr. Hoffmann
out. He was escorted to a more decent-looking shipping container,
which inside looked like a very nice office. Mr. Hoffmann's eyes took a
minute adjusting to the brightness.

On the back wall was a bulletin board. A heavy wooden desk with
wrought iron handles stood in front, with a leather chair behind it. On
the desk was a desk lamp, couple stacked books with a pen mug on top,
an open binder, and laptop. The chair spun around.

"You may go," he told the guards, in a cold, hard voice with no accent.
He pushed his chair back, revealing more openly photographs on his
bulletin board.

Mr. Hoffmann sucked in his breath. On it were every member of his
family, past and present.

Chapter Thirteen - Worthy Enough

THE MAN POINTED TO Patrick's photograph. "This is your son. Patrick Hunter Hoffmann. He is married to Sarah Isobel Lorenzi. They have a young son, *Benjamin*. He is thirty-two years old, and works as a Marine. He did his training very well. Almost *too* well. As if it was just a stroll through times square. You home-

schooled him and his siblings all their lives. Why?" he asked in a very commanding voice.

Inwardly, Mr. Hoffmann scowled at him. *A pox on you! And the UN,* thought he.

"You realize I could have you executed right known?"

Mr. Hoffmann shrugged innocently, though inside his heart was racing. The man recoiled.

His eyes turned fiery angry.

"I will get answers. You will give them to me."

Mr. Hoffmann smiled and pointed at the man.

"You think you will-" he lowered his finger and began to shake his head, "But you won't."

"We will see. GUARDS!!" he screamed, which brought them running. "Whip this man fifty times."

One of them smiled. "Yes, Officer Igor."

Igor? Mr. Hoffmann k nitted h is b row i n c onfusion. Th e officers dragged him outside.

———————

THE MORNING DAWNED. Mr. Hoffmann was tied to a post in the middle of the camp. His back was practically ripped open. Other prisoners looked sympathetically at him, but lacked the courage to help.

Officer Igor smugly walked by. "Would you like to have another talk, sir?"

With a clear soft voice, Mr. Hoffmann began to sing Martin Luther's famous hymn 'A Mighty Fortress Is Our God'

Officer Igor growled softly when Mr. Hoffmann strongly sang verses 10 - 15, speaking of how the devil will not prevail.

———————

"WHY ISN'T IT WORKING?" the thin man asked the fat woman, Delilah.

"This is very strange. I can't see a thing," she replied.

"What will we say to the officer?"

———————

"WAKE UP SLEEPYHEADS!!" Martha rang the family's bronze dinner bell loudly, which produced an 'angelic' sound.

Teddy, the King Shepherd, looked at her from his rug by the door and yawned.

The sounds roused the others, and one by one they slowly got up.

"Good morning!" she said to them in a singsong voice.

Susan, the younger boys, and Elizabeth looked down curiously from the loft at the sight of the Green Berets.

"Morn, Effy," Patrick said from his bed.

Elizabeth and the others gasped and turned. "Pat!" they exclaimed in disbelief, and ran to give him a hug.

Sarah appeared from the bathroom. "What's all the commotion up here?" she asked groggily.

"We didn't know the boys and Green Berets came here!" Susan cried, jumping happily in the big bed.

Sarah turned her head to the other queen-sized bed. The others turned as well.

Daniel jumped in, the others close behind him. Benjamin was the first to see the face of the body.

"Granddame!" he said, loud enough for five stories below to hear. The others gaped as they were wrapped in Mrs. Hoffmann's arms. Tears of gratitude and thankfulness streamed down Mrs. Hoffmann's face.

Patrick and Sarah watched the reunion with tears in their own eyes. Samuel and George had already gone downstairs, but along with Martha and the dogs, came back up. Dakota and Nellie exchanged surprised glances. Nell looked down, sorry she was angry Mrs. Hoffmann was alive, and her own mother was not.

Mrs. Hoffmann disengaged herself from them.

As they were hugging thoughts ran through Susan's mind, unlike the others, who were basking in the moment.

"Father? Where is he?" she asked.

Mrs. Hoffmann sighed. "I don't know, sweetheart. We can pray. Not worry."

They all gulped.

"Now, why don't we all get ready for our day and *pray*?"

They all nodded and ran off. The ones who knew already she was there stayed, since they were dressed unlike the others.

Mrs. Hoffmann threw off her sheet and went to the clothes cupboard.

She took out black combat boots, matching pants, and a black quilted vest. The others had on similar clothing. She then wordlessly went to the bathroom.

Elizabeth and Martha began cooking breakfast; scrambled eggs to be served with beef jerky. It took them less than thirty minutes to cook the eggs. During breakfast, the boys and Marines related to Elizabeth, Sue, the younger boys, and the McFarlanes their plans. After breakfast, the Hoffmanns and Marines had a time of prayer, each person respectfully saying prayers in their minds.

Dear Lord, Susan prayed fervently, and with passion, *thank you for all the good times you have given us. Help us trust you even in these hard times. We rejoice that we are...* she choked on tears. *That we are worthy enough to go through this tribulation. Amen.*

Father, Nellie said, feeling ashamed. *I'm sorry for feeling jealous. Not just know, but for other times. When I have lusted for all the things the Hoffmanns had. But now, even still, after they've lost everything, sentimental items, their grand house, and have no idea what is happening to their father, I feel angry and vile against them. Please forgive me. I know they have dealt with many more trials and tribulations... but please give me the strength to not feel this way. Help me and Dak make it through this time of darkness...and glorify you. Amen.*

God, you know I'm not good at eloquent prayers, but please protect us all. These children, the older ones, me and my men, and anybody else that believes in Your word and marvelous truth. Amen. This was General Conner's simple prayer, and the other Marines' prayers ran along similar lines, except John.

Lord, he prayed with great conviction, *right now I ask that You would show Your truth to the many people of this country, and of this world. Allow them to repent of their hideous and evil sins, to You, who ever knee will bow down before. Amen.*

Before any of them knew it, two hours of prayer time sped by, but the time had not been spent in vain.

The Marines, and the older boys then hastily did the few things needed to prepare for an unwelcome adventure.

"I'm coming too," Mrs. Hoffmann announced.

Her boys glanced at each other. "Mother," Patrick said with as much respect as he could muster, "You shouldn't come. It's dangerous. You could get hurt really bad. It's safer here."

"I know that, my son, and I know that you're thinking of my safety, but it will be no more dangerous than any other scenario I have dealt with in the last forty-eight hours," she said convincingly. She saw that Samuel was about to open his mouth to back up his brother. "And if you don't want me to come, I will be forced to do it anyway," she added.

The boys looked at each other again, a silent message conveying between it; *There's no use in trying to talk her out of it.*

Patrick nodded reluctantly. "Fine."

"Good. It's settled then."

"But...Mommy..." Daniel said slowly, not wishing her to go.

"Dan, dear, I feel that it is my responsibility to help your brothers, and find out if your father is alright," she explained.

"But..." he pouted, "isn't it your re-bon-sibilty," –here he hesitated over the word- "to look after us... here, too?"

"Dan," Nellie said, crouching down to be the boy's height, "That is true, but since your sisters can take care of you just as well as your mother can, she has a higher duty to go with them."

The others nodded in agreement. Daniel seemed to be working this out in his little brain. Finally, his pout left, and he walked over and gave his mother a hug. As they hugged, Mrs. Hoffmann mouthed, "Thank you," to Nellie.

As Dak had not said a word all morn long, Nellie longed to speak with him in private.

The girls also hugged Mrs. Hoffmann one by one.

As they got ready, Susan seemed to be thinking their plan through. "So...you're just going to drive through town looking for FEMA camps? That doesn't seem optimal."

Mrs. Hoffmann smiled. "Of course not. I'm going to sneak in with the boys through the sewers, then act as a normal person walking about town. I'll be in communication with the boys via our comms line, relaying information when I spot a FEMA camp," she clarified.

"But...camera's..." Sarah's words trailed off. "You'll need a disguise!"

"But...we'll just have to make due with what we got," Patrick replied.

Dakota looked up. "Hold on!" he cried, and marched to the loft and came down with what looked like a wooden art kit.

Everyone waited in expectant silence as he slammed the case on the island.

They all gasped as they were faced with a variety of makeup, wigs, hair dye, and different types of clothes.

"What on earth?" Nellie asked. "So this is where all my stuff went?!"

Dakota flashed her a slightly guilty grin.

Benjamin giggled. "What's it for, Dak?" he asked.

"I've also had a thing for disguises," he replied. "Me and my buddies liked to completely change our appearances."

"Thank the Lord!" Susan exclaimed.

"We need to make you as different from *you* as possible, without it seeming that way, of course. Hair is thing that most people identify with, and," he looked at the girls with their shorter hair cuts, "Since brown is pretty much the most common hair color, it makes no sense to change it...But we can shorten it to about shoulder length," he simplified.

"That was me and Augustine's plan anyway in a SHTF situation," she said, in full agreement.

"As I am a dude, who did the cutting before?" he queried.

"I did," Sarah replied.

"Alright. Eyes are another thing most people identify with...so..." he pulled a small case out of his large case, "we need to change that."

Chapter Fourteen – Morse Code Message

DAKOTA AND SARAH STOOD back and admired their handiwork.

Mrs. Hoffmann looked much different. Her short hair was in a simple plait, she wore casual sweatpants, a simple striped T-shirt under a dark hoodie, and her eyes were a sterling gray unlike her natural brown eyes. She still wore her combat boots, which blended in with her casual outfit.

"Where's Granddame?" Benjamin asked when he came out of the bathroom. Susan pointed, and the boy took a big breath.

"You look so changed!" Martha exclaimed. "I don't know if I like it," she said.

"Well, looks don't really matter, Mae, in this situation," Patrick explained.

"I know," she defensively replied.

"Are we ready?" the General asked.

"Yes."

MRS. HOFFMANN DID HER best to quiet the swelling in her heart. She and the men had taken the same route into Chicago as they had before, only not getting out near the stadium. When Mrs. Hoffmann turned left, if they could the men turned left. People had finally came out of their apartments and tried to figure out what was going on.

Work was put on hold, schools shut down, and grocery stores stopped receiving deliveries.

She came to West 63rd street. Her intense gaze fell on O'Hare International Airport. People had gathered on the outskirts of it. The subway tracks, entrance, were not crowded, there was a small crowd of about a hundred people. Her steps quickened a little bit. She slowed when she finally neared the entrance. Why were people not *inside*?

A voice suddenly boomed over the loudspeakers. "Please remove yourselves from near the entrance. You are in danger here."

People, of course, fled from the entrance, and Mrs. Hoffmann for show, more than anything, joined along.

There was something they wanted to hide. But what was it? As the crowd was almost very completely away from the airport, in the mayhem, Mrs. Hoffmann slid out and hid behind a dumpster.

I hope the cameras haven't spotted me, she thought nervously. "Patrick?" she whispered into the comms line.

"Yes?"

"I'm going to investigate what they want to hide in the airport," she clarified.

"Oh Mama, be careful," Martha's voice cut in, surprising everyone that she had been listening in.

"I know. But there is seriously something they want to hide. I have t-," she was cut short as she heard commotion from the back of the airport. She crept out of her less than desirable hiding place and hugged the wall.

She ran back when a *thud-thud* sound of combat boots started her way.

Father, please help me! Mrs. Hoffmann slid as far back behind the dumpster as possible, then quickly summoned the courage to peek around the side. She stifled a huge gasp and crept back. After she was certain no-one became alerted to her presence, she hurriedly whispered into the comms line. "Saw all female division of peacekeepers."

"What?" came Samuel's voice.

"That doesn't make sense," Patrick said, "Even the UN knows men have more stamina than women."

"Maybe they're just the ones patrolling the street," George suggested.

"Maybe. But that can't be what the UN is trying to hide. Seems to me like they would be proud of it instead," Mrs. Hoffmann said. "I'm going to continue sneaking."

"Right. Just be careful," Patrick agreed.

Mrs. Hoffmann slid against the wall and in a sneak-run went close to the heavy barbed wire fence.

Her heart jumped in her throat. Half-shocked to death, she tried to stable her nerves and ran back again to her hiding place.

"Pa-," she swallowed, "-Patrick?"

"Yeah?"

"I just saw a statue of the pope"

"WHAT?" MARTHA SAID, the word drawn out.

"Oh no way," Sarah groaned.

"What is that?" Daniel asked.

"The pope is a man that wants to reestablish the Catholic church's rule over the world. Put back in a feudalistic system," Elizabeth replied.

"Why?"

"Evil has no end, little brother."

Daniel absorbed the information, then went back to his picture Bible.

On the radio, Patrick took a few moments to think.

"Are you positive?"

Mrs. Hoffmann felt annoyed at the question, and reigned herself in. "Yes."

"Why would they...?" George left the question unfinished.

"Maybe the pope wants to rule Chicago," came Elizabeth's voice.

"Are you all listening in?" Samuel wondered out loud.

An affirmative came over the line. Noise from above was heard by the men, and they quickly got in position.

"Mother?" Patrick asked over the line. No response.

A body jumped down the hole. "Patrick?"

"Mother!"

"Wheest! (hush!)! They're still up there!" she cried, almost falling into the water.

John bent down, and Peter Jr. Climbed on his back and shut the lid.

"Let's keep going," the General said.

THE HAM RADIO SUDDENLY beeped a morse code message, and Martha hurried to remember the sequences.

She was on guard duty while the others slept, and when she had written down the message, her jaw drooped and she wondered whether or not she had translated correctly.

She swallowed her shock, and climbed up the rope and shook Sarah and Elizabeth. They had just fallen asleep again.

"What is it?" Sarah asked sleepily, while Elizabeth rubbed her eyes.

"It was a national emergency alert. Uh...Trump is dead. He was assassinated while Putin was at the White House. Apparently the assassin was a member of the security detail for Putin," Martha sighed deeply. "And Pence is president now. And he's in league with the globalists. It seems as if they're attacking all at once."

Elizabeth rolled over and began breathing deeply.

"You'd better tell the boys," Sarah instructed.

Martha nodded and slid down the rope.

"ARE YOU SERIOUS?" PATRICK couldn't believe his ears.

"I wouldn't try to play a practical joke on you, Patrick. What good would that do?" Martha said sardonically.

"You don't have any more information than that?" Samuel asked.

"It was in morse code. If I missed anything..."

"I see. Well, we haven't come across any FEMA camps, yet. I'll let you know when we do," Patrick said.

Chapter Fifteen - Your Majesty

A SECRETARY WITH SHOULDER-length deep brown hair came in hesitantly. "Uh...Your Majesty, My Lady, I bring urgent news from the states," she said, her British accent cutting through the air.

Queen Elizabeth the second of the United Kingdom looked up from her silver tea set. She had been in converse with the uppity Meghan, Duchess of Sussex. "Ah, yes. I have been expecting word from there." The old woman set down her tea cup, waiting for the secretary to speak. "Well, Angelica, go on," the Queen said rather impatiently.

"We are getting reports, Your Majesty, that a bomb has been dropped on the Washington D.C area."

The Duchess and the Queen exchanged looks. The Queen's face showed neither surprise at the news nor concern. "Hmm. Contact me with Theresa May."

Angelica, a young woman in her thirties, slowly walked away, mind spinning, grey eyes bothered. *Why didn't Her Majesty show surprise at my statement? Nor did she show any surprise when I told her that Chicago was know being run by UN peacekeepers. Oh, Lord! Is it possible that she is in league with those people and their agenda?*

Angelica gasped in shock when she slammed into somebody else. "I'm terribly sorry," she said apologetically as she continued to walk through the golden halls of the Tower of London to her small office.

Oh, Father, please help me make sense of it all. I feel like a sheep surrounded by five hundred wolves, with no way to escape, and they just waiting to devour me.

After what seemed like an eternity, Angelica finally reached her office door, and hurriedly entered the sanctuary.

The walls of her office held only a watercolor painting of some flowers here and there. Her desk was an old and worn wooden desk which had been in the fortress many years, and on top was her laptop, official computer, a cute stationery notebook, and an acrylic pen holder. Also there was a fixed-line telephone.

She pushed back her office chair and sank onto it. After only a couple of seconds, she opened a desk drawer and took out an official looking binder. She flipped a few of the pages, then stopped when she found the one she wanted.

She dialed a number quickly and waited. "Prime Minister's office."

"David? This is Angelica Clarke-"

"I'll get the Prime Minister on right away."

"Thank you, David," Angelica replied. She did something to connect her phone to the Queen's. "Your Majesty," she said and waited for a response.

"Yes?"

"Prime Minister Theresa should be on any minute now."

"Very well, Angelica."

Angelica's telephone beeped to tell her that her phone had been disconnected so that she could not listen in. But, Angelica knew that she could listen in. After a couple moments of hesitation, Angelica opened a drawer and pulled out a slim, old fashioned, voice recorder.

She did something to gain access into the Prime Minister's and the Queen's Conversation. And just as voice came through, she hit the button on the recorder.

"-So are we to go through with the plan, Majesty?"

"Of course. It is time for America to pay for what they did to us. They stopped us from ruling those lands, made us poor, and humiliated us in front of all the world."

"Shall I contact our allies?"

"Yes. Inform France, Canada, the US, and the Vatican that we have received information that North Korea sent that missile."

"And that we should all do what is best for the world... destroy North Korea once and for all."

Angelica gaped, and quickly disconnected from the conversation and she also hit the button on the recorder. Her breath came in ragged gasps, and she knew that her life was in danger. She quickly picked up her designer black tote bag, stuffed in her laptop, hid her recorder in a hidden pocket of her purse, and strode in a hasty walk out the door.

The sentences she just heard kept repeating in her head. *"Destroy North Korea once and for all...Time for America to pay for all they did to us...Shall I inform our Allies...France, the US, Canada, the Vatican...tell them we received information that North Korea sent that missile."*

Angelica took a deep breath and pressed the elevator button with her knuckle. *What am I going to do with this information?* She thought nervously. *To whom shall I give it? Infowars? The Veritas Project? Both? Oh, God, help me in my desperate hour!*

The elevator door opened and she walked in, nervously noting that her companion was the castle's security manager and supervisor.

"Miss Clarke," the man said.

Angelica licked her dry lips. "Mr. Wright."

"Being dismissed early today?" he asked.

Angelica knew she had to respond. "I'm not feeling well," she said. That was the absolute truth. Regrettably, she looked at her clothing. A pencil skirt and high heels were not great things to fight in or run in.

Angelica let out a small breath of relief as the elevator doors slid open. She had walked about a metre (3 feet) when she heard footfalls behind her.

Before she had a chance to blink, Angelica's arms were behind her back and her wrists were held together my handcuffs and her tote bag was vigorously being searched.

Mr. Wright exclaimed angrily and let her bag fall to the ground, when suddenly Angelica saw her laptop on the hard floor, cracked and broken.

"Are you kidding me? What is the meaning of this atrocity?" she asked, not about what she knew was the reason for her detainment, but about why they treated her laptop so rudely.

She had saved many years for the laptop.

"Take her away!" Mr. Wright yelled to the guards.

———

ANGELICA AWOKE IN A shipping container, with bunks lining the walls. The last thing she remembered was being shoved into a jet.

"Where am I?" she asked out loud.

"You're in a Walmart in Chicago," a voice answered.

Without meaning to, Angelica yelped in fright to actually hear someone answer her. "What? Chicago? Who are you?"

"The name's Augustine Hoffmann. I would shake your hand if I could, but it's so dark in here, I have no idea where you are."

"Oh. Well, hello, sire. I'm Angelica Clarke."

"I'm guessing you don't have a clue what's going on?" Mr. Hoffmann asked.

Angelica nodded, then foolishly realized that was meaningless if the man couldn't see here. "Yes, that's correct."

"Well, this place is a fortified Walmart run by Federal Emergency Management Agency Agents and United Nations peacekeepers. You're in a shipping container with bunks and other prisoners. People here are 'enemies of the state' and are detained, interrogated, and, if they don't comply...are tortured," Mr. Hoffmann gave a little sigh. "Like me," he said softly.

"Torture?" Angelica ventured hesitantly.

"Yes. They many whip you, half-hang you, or beat you with a bat. Who knows. We can only trust the Lord," Mr. Hoffmann replied.

"Are you a heretic, Sire?" Angelica asked.

"What?"

"A heretic. A Christian. A Jew. Not believing in Roman Catholicism. A heretic."

"Huh. Well, yes, I understand what a heretic is, but your question took me by surprise. And, yes. I am a Christian," Mr. Hoffmann replied.

Normally, Angelica would be extremely overjoyed to hear someone say they were a Christian, especially in such circumstances. But the situation she experienced earlier had hardened her heart, making her extremely more cautious than usual.

"Really, Sire?" she asked Mr. Hoffmann, obviously not knowing he was an extremely devout man. Angelica's mind scrambled for a Biblical version of a test. "If I walked around in stretchy pants, would you say I was a Christian?"

"Certainly not!" Mr. Hoffmann indignantly responded. Not Susan, Elizabeth, or Martha had ever walked out of the house wearing 'yoga' pants.

"What about shorts over the knee?"

"That's about worse!"

"What's does John 16:33 say?"

"'In this world you will have tribulation, but be of good cheer, I have overcome the world,'" Mr. Hoffmann replied without hesitation.

Angelica was not yet satisfied. "Tell me the first 10 books of the Old Testament."

And so it was that (sorry! Forgive me for the Bible pun!) Mr. Hoffmann told her, and Angelica was convinced of his sincerity.

"I find it interesting that you asked me those kind of questions," Mr. Hoffmann told her. "Do they mean something to you?"

"Yes," Angelica answered, laughing softly. "My great-great grandfather, in my ancestral town of Lampeter, Wales, wanted to make it illegal in 1881 for any woman to wear anything above the ankle line, or anything form-fitting. Unfortunately, that was not to be the case. He, that is, Grandfather Vincent, also went through many tribulations in his life...and at his funeral, that verse, John 16:33, was in a frame, cross-stitched my Grandmother Louise."

"Wow," Mr. Hoffmann said, impressed. "That's very cool. I guess that story was passed down through the years?"

"Precisely, Mr. Hoffmann. That's the main reason my family has always prized modesty, "Angelica replied.

"Can you speak Welsh?" Mr. Hoffmann asked suddenly.

Angelica laughed. "Uh, no. I wish I did, but no. My father moved from Welsh to England for better job opportunities, leaving his brother and his family as the only ones to continue the Clarke name."

Mr. Hoffmann yawned. "Let's try t- "

The shipping container door opened, revealing the rising sun. Mr. Hoffmann and Angelica grimaced at the light.

"Huh!" a Chinese officer scoffed. "Two of our prisoners conversing together, huh? Well, you'll both die together!" his voice matched well his body; greedy and brusque.

He and another peacekeeper hoisted Angelica to her feet and shoved her out of the shipping container.

"Hope you're ready for your interrogation. Is everything alright because you met Meghan?" the officer said tauntingly as they shoved her out of the shipping container.

"Why should I be proud to have met that woman? She's not the as pretty as everybody makes her out to be, and she's dumber than a brick. Everything's alright because I know God."

"Ha!" the officer laughed evilly. "Well, you certainly have heart!"

Help her, God, Mr. Hoffmann prayed as she went out of view.

Chapter Sixteen - Civility

———

ANGELICA, TREMBLING fearfully, was brought to Officer Igor, the same man that had interrogated Mr. Hoffmann.

He had the same strategy with Angelica; intimidate her by the amount of information he had on her.

"This is your father, Jack Clarke," he pointed to a photo on his bulletin board.

Angelica stayed silent, not trusting herself to speak.

"He is dead. Death was natural. This your mother, *Angie* Clarke. She is still alive, living happily in a condominium in Croydon, England. I bet she's not going to be happy very soon," he added, with a piercing look at Angelica.

Angelica swallowed.

"This is your father's brother, Jake Clarke," he continued. "He lives in Lampeter, Wales, with his wife, Lacey May, and their 3 children. Jason, James, and Joshua. Your family has been very distant with them since you left Wales...

"It's a shame Jake didn't approve of his brother leaving...But...maybe he was actually very intelligent. It's a very *great* shame that he's going to have to pay for his brother's mistake, and his niece's. You didn't like boarding school, apparently, because you arrived home after the first week. 'I miss my mommy and daddy. It's not that I don't wanna be here but...I don't feel well here and I miss my parents," Officer Igor said in a childish voice.

How in the entire world does he know what I said to that wretched princi-pal??? Angelica thought angrily.

"Your superiors deemed you mentally weak, and sent you home."

"Miss," he said, leaning over the top of his chair. "I'm going to be very straight with you. If you don't provide me with the information I ask for, I will have you executed immediately. Is that clear? So answer me."

"Why did you listen in?" Officer Igor queried.

Don't be snappy Angelica, she told herself. *Keep a stony silence, girl!*

Officer Igor waited a few seconds. He got up and walked outside.

After at least five minutes, Angelica began to wonder if she could es-cape. *Don't be foolish! This place is surrounded by guards.*

Finally, Officer Igor returned, bringing with him another officer.

"Sergey, you may sit," Igor said.

'Sergey' was fat, had a very Russian beard, and was older than Igor.

Officer Igor repeated his question to Angelica. Still she said nothing.

Igor lost his patience and screamed out the question.

Sergey frowned, nudged his compatriot, and muttered a few words in Russian.

Angrily Igor retorted, and Angelica was almost positive she heard something like, "Girl... don't...rough...civil....be. What? ...Why? You're... unstable... mentally."

Don't be rough, be civil.

Why? You're crazy?

You're mentally unstable!

Is that what they're saying? Angelica thought, thoroughly befuddled. *Wait a minute...*

Officer Igor turned back to her. "Are you a legal citizen of England?" he asked.

"Yes," Angelica answered strategically to see whether or not her assumption was correct.

"They why did you betray your country?" Officer Sergey asked in a thick accent.

"I didn't," Angelica replied.

"Then why are you here?" Igor said.

"Were you...mind-controlled?" asked Sergey.

"Yes," Angelica replied.

"Poor girl," Sergey muttered with a glance at his compatriot, who's expression had becoming more piercing.

"You're both fools!" Angelica suddenly cried. "Did you really think I wouldn't understand the game of good cop, bad cop?! Couldn't you come with anything better?!?"

Igor and Sergey looked at each other. "It's too bad you didn't play along. Now we'll have to play another game, but it's more...grueling."

———————

ANGELICA GASPED, EXERTED from her pain. She had been half-hanged more than five times, each time the pain becoming more and more intolerable. Each time she became unconscious, then the officers would cut her down and drag her to her bunk. The other female detainees would help her as best as they could, having nothing comforting themselves.

Slowly Angelica's eyelids drooped closed, and she fought tensely for air, but the pressure around her neck only tightened, and Angelica's self-will was dropping. She did not know how much longer she could hold out.

———

ANGELICA ONCE AGAIN awoke at her bunk. Her feet hurt and her throat ached.

She sighed. She was feeling very bad. It was worse than having a temporary computer virus, which always spiked Angelica's nerves.

A woman in a bunk across from her looked at her curiously. The woman had small, brown piercing eyes, and her hair seemed much too long for her body.

"What do they want from you?" she asked.

Maybe it was her imagination, but Angelica thought she heard a slight accent.

"Intelligence," she answered, knowing that practically everyone there the UN hoped to gain 'intelligence' from.

Mr. Hoffmann noticed the exchange and went over to Angelica's bunk.

Covering his one hand with the other, Mr. Hoffmann prayed that Angelica knew ASL (American Sign Language). He spelled out: DON'T TRUST HER!

After he did that a couple of times, Angelica's gaze finally shifted to him.

The woman was taken out by some peacekeepers, giving her and Mr. Hoffmann the perfect opportunity to 'talk'.

Mr. Hoffmann led her to his bunk, where it was more sheltered from prying eyes.

WHY? Angelica asked.

SPY. Mr. Hoffmann simply explained, then he added, SHE'S NEW. STAY STRONG, ANGELICA. THE TORTURE WILL BE OVER SOON. MY KIDS WILL FREE US.

HOW?

THEY WILL. I TRAINED THEM WELL. I WILL BRING YOU ALONG. I HAVE A FEELING YOU HAVE VERY DAMAGING INFORMATION.

Angelica frowned. HOW WILL THEY FREE US?

It was Mr. Hoffmann's turned to frown. WHAT? THAT DOESN'T MATTER. TELL ME THE INFORMATION YOU HAVE.

Angelica hesitated... I DON'T KNOW.

GIRL, DO YOU WANT TO STAY HERE? I'M SORRY, BUT IF YOU'RE INFORMATION IS IRRELEVANT, I WILL LEAVE YOU HERE.

That broke the line for Angelica. THE QUEEN OF ENGLAND IS HELPING DESTROY THIS COUNTRY. SHE WANTS TO RULE IT AND MAKE YOU PAY FOR KICKING THEIR BUTTS. I WAS ONE OF HER SECRETARIES. I LISTENED IN ON ONE OF HER TALKS WITH PRIME MINISTER THERESA MAY. I RECORDED IT. BUT I HAVE NO IDEA WERE THE RECORDING IS.

MR. HOFFMANN PAUSED. OKAY. WELL, YOU'RE COMING WITH. HAVE YOU EVER USED A FIREARM?

Angelica gasped loudly. And she hastily looked around to see if anyone had noticed. They hadn't. They were focused on another prisoner being shoved in the shipping container.

It was a young woman with Titian hair, a sturdy frame, and her teeth was set. Her name was Tabetha Lee.

Her black leather jacket was dirty, her hair was matted, and her feet stumbled seemingly constantly.

Suddenly, she grabbed the arm of one her captor's and dug her elbow into the man's elbow socket, while pulling his wrist simultaneously. At the same time, she slammed him into her other captor, who dropped his rifle and banged into the wall, slumping down. Tabetha grabbed the rifle and sprinted out.

SARAH HAD BEEN CONVERSING with her husband and his brothers while they searched for Mr. Hoffmann.

"We need to get," she told them. "It's becoming just too dangerous to remain here," she paused. "I have an idea for speeding up finding Father. Go to the nearest Walmart."

"But," George countered, "You never know where a FEMA camp might hang out. It could be at a library, or a phone store, we just don't know, that's why we have this strategy."

"Don't be a dumb-brick," Sarah said unapologetically. Our research has shown that either a Walmart or a stadium is most likely to be used as a FEMA camp. If it doesn't work, then resume with your original plan. But your original plan *isn't* working. Time to try something else. Patrick?"

Patrick nodded. "Tell us the address," he agreed.

———————

"SARAH WAS ABSOLUTELY right. Thank God. But...let's hope your father's here," Mrs. Hoffmann said, leaning against a bus stop post and staring at the imposing structure before her.

A high black chained-link fence with sharp barbed wire on top challengingly faced the outside, detaining people on the inside. Shipping containers created a courtyard around the actual Walmart entrance.

FEMA and UN logos were on the fence, spitting in the face of justice and truth.

"All right. Stay up there, Mother," Patrick said. "We'll devise a strategy. Is public transportation still working?" he asked.

"Yes. I saw a bus with practically no people inside," Mrs. Hoffmann replied.

"Good. Act as if you are waiting on a bus," Patrick suggested.

"Men," he said speaking to his brothers and the Green Berets, "Walter, John, take up strategic sniper positions around the Walmart. Abe, Luke, do the same thing but on the ground. The rest of us will storm the place once you and the others are in position. I known I probably don't need to say this, but...there's no reason to show any civility."

Chapter Seventeen - Haste

———

CHARLEY'S CAMERA BEEPED. He wheeled around and studied the screen. There was a woman leaning against a bus post, lips moving but seemingly talking to no-one. She wore a hoodie, bulky boots, and had short hair pulled back in a messy braid.

Charley typed in a few words. Photographs of missing prisoners came up, comparing the woman's photo to others.

Suddenly, the computer stopped scrolling and stopped. A photo of Mrs. Hoffmann and her disguise was next to each other. "Same facial shape," the voice said. Charley laughed evilly.

"Boys, I got a mission for you," he said into his walkie-talkie.

———

"ALRIGHT. IS EVERYBODY in position?" Patrick asked.

"Roger," he got from everyone.

"Good. Walter?"

He and John had climbed up a building with bear claws that slipped over the hand. It could dig into hard surfaces such as brick and stone.

John stood up from lying on the roof. He grabbed something in one hand. Walter stood up as well. They both aimed at two different look-out posts.

"One, two, three!" John shouted, springing forward at the same time and letting fly his grip.

"BANG!"

The lookouts went up in smoke. Instantly the gate opened and out came angry peacekeepers, who knelt down and aimed at Walter and John, who were very unsheltered.

Something whistled at the peacekeepers: shots from Abe and Luke, who were rushing forward. Shots unexpectedly came from *inside* the compound, making the men look confusedly at each other.

A couple of peacekeepers had hastily went up the remaining lookout towers, but turned back at the sounds inside.

Mrs. Hoffmann pulled out her Glock 19 and hurried toward the gate, where it hadn't yet been closed, and Abe and Luke quickly joined up with her and rushed inside.

———————

MR. HOFFMANN AND ANGELICA gasped at the scene, and Mr. Hoffmann hurriedly went to the unconscious peacekeepers, taking off their armor quickly and handing Angelica a handgun and ear plugs. In horror she took it. She and Mr. Hoffmann darted out, leaving the other prisoners speechless.

Angelica groaned and tripped in the concert, skinning her shins and bruising her ankle. She knew time was essential. To her everything else had gone blurry. She got up and struggled fiercely to take off her strapped high-heels.

Finally, she tossed them off and ran for the entrance, with Mr. Hoffmann nowhere in sight. Suddenly, two of the watchtowers went up in flames, forcing Angelica to cover her ears as she ran. Her feet hurt even worse running and her stockings snagged on the ground.

Mr. Hoffmann appeared, and drew her to the side of one of the shipping containers.

"Stay here!" he screamed and ran off.

Angelica rolled up in a ball and prayed fiercely.

MR. HOFFMANN RAN RIGHT back to the area where he had been held captive. He shot a couple of peacekeepers along the way, but the compound provided numerous places to hide.

Quickly he sneaked to where the actual Walmart building was. A number of peacekeepers darted out and Mr. Hoffmann decided not to engage. He snuck to the entrance before taking a Grenade from his 'borrowed' vest and tossing it through the doors, then he ran for the compound exit.

Chaos was an understatement.

The dissidents were going crazy, trying to overpower their captors, while their captors went savage and needed back up from the actual Walmart building.

Because of the fact that the other officers were busy trying to control the prisoners, it provided Mr. Hoffmann with ample conditions for his escape.

He was halfway to the exit when a Titian head popped out from behind a UN armored vehicle.

"BANG!"

The other watchtowers went up in flame.

Then he saw something very surprising, three figures rushing through and quickly conversing with the Titian girl who had almost reached the exit.

———

ABE, LUKE, AND MRS. Hoffmann had burst in the compound when they were startlingly faced with a young girl.

"Tabetha!" Luke exclaimed, with Mrs. Hoffmann and Abe looking at him perplexingly.

"You know her?" Abe asked quickly.

"Yes," Luke replied without clarifying. "What are you doing here?" he asked her.

"I was captured, betrayed by a distant relative. What are you doing here?"

"We came for her husband," Luke replied with a nod in Mrs. Hoffmann's direction.

———

ANGELICA WATCHED AS the foursome conversed hastily. She then peeked around the corning to look for Mr. Hoffmann. It was very loud, and the air still smelled of smoke. He saw her peek, and motioned her to go to the foursome.

Angelica hesitated then bolted towards them. They raised their weapons suspiciously.

"Who are you?" Abe immediately asked.

"She was a prisoner, I saw her," Tabetha said.

"My name's Angelica Clarke an-" Mrs. Hoffmann sprang forward, instantly recognizing the face of an approaching figure.

"Augustine!"

Angelica, Tabetha, and the men's jaws all dropped.

"Amazing," Luke finally said.

"What is going on?" Angelica said nervously. "That man befriended me."

"He's her husband," Luke explained.

The girls' jaws dropped again.

A bullet whizzing past them awoke them to the reality of their present situation. The girls looked over their shoulder and gasped.

UN peacekeepers were about 5 yards away.

"Don't move," the leader said menacingly. Abe's jaw went lower.

"The man from the control room!" he exclaimed. "We shoulda killed you."

"You should've," Charley agreed. "But you didn't. Drop the weapons and turn around.

The men around him went lump. He looked back, were Walter and John were, and to the sides, were Patrick and the other Green Berets were coming.

Before he turned, he himself went lump.

"Well, that's ironic," Mrs. Hoffmann said walking hand in hand with Mr. Hoffmann.

She was referring to the fact that Abe had killed him.

The boys and Green Berets abruptly appeared. "Father!" the boys said in unison, and darted forward.

"Ach! Careful!" Mr. Hoffmann said as there was a large family hug. The boys backed away, frowning.

"He was tortured for information because the UN thought he was part of Chicago Underground," Mrs. Hoffmann clarified, with a glance at Tabetha. She gasped and looked down.

"Oh, no!" came Susan's voice through the comms line.

John and Walter jumped up. "GUYS! GET OUTTA THERE! YOU'VE GOT A HELICOPTER COMING STRAIGHT FOR YOU!" John screamed at the top of his lungs.

"Come on!" Patrick hollered. They ran from the compound exit, then UN armored vehicles appeared from both sides of the street. Patrick and them ran across, through cut-throughs and yards. He looked around for a means of escape. There was none.

Angelica groaned. She was slowing down and her feet were bleeding. Mr. Hoffmann looked around, and with an angry mutter handed his wife his rifle and lifted Angelica up.

"Always be prepared," he muttered angrily.

Angelica bit her lip, feeling weak and foolish.

The helicopter approached them and started firing. Tabetha stopped running and aimed and fired her AK-47 at it. It was a big target, but was not close enough for the shot to do any real damage.

"ZOOM"

FATHER AND SON FLASHED each other tense looks. Flicking off their bear claws down, they then jumped down the 15 feet. Feeling only slightly bruised, they hastily got up and ran after the Hoffmanns and their fellow Green Berets. They quickly caught up with them.

"Where are we going?" Walter yelled, wanting to add a curse word but not.

"I have no idea," Patrick replied honestly.

"We need a plan!" Tabetha exclaimed.

"Where are you?!" came Martha's voice through the comms line.

"Uh..." George looked around for a road sign. "West 35th Street!"

There was a sound of shuffling of paper and muffled voices.

"When you reach the end of the street, turn left!" Elizabeth urgently instructed.

"Patrick?" Samuel said. "You got that?"

"Got it!" he replied.

They continued running through the alley until they come to the end of it, and made a sharp left, bullets whizzing after them. Eventually Mr. Hoffmann began to tire with the additional wait he was carrying.

A man came out of a building and noticed the parade and observed quickly. "Wait!"

He ran over to the suspicious group. "Wait," he repeated. He pulled something out of his backpack. "That girl needs shoes. You'll never make it if she doesn't," he handed it to Mr. Hoffmann who had set Angelica down. It was a pair of white, lace-up sneakers.

"Thank you?!" Angelica asked as she put it on.

"Godspeed!"

Angelica finished putting on the hard shoes and then they resumed their running.

"When you reach the end, look for a sewer spot. You'll have to fight to go all of you to get in," Martha said.

"But Martha!" Samuel objected, "This is all railroad!"

There was a sound of urgent voices and then Elizabeth's voice. "However possible go to the high school!"

Chapter Eighteen – Give Yourself Up

———

THEY ALL RAN AS FAST as they could, and they finally reached the high school.

"What now, Effy?" Mrs. Hoffmann asked.

"Look around the campus for a sewer drain! Or some type of cover!"

They all frantically looked around, but saw nothing.

The realization that the helicopter was getting closer and closer came into view.

They moved to a more sheltered area of the brick campus.

"There!" Tabetha pointed.

It was out in the open, with little cover.

"Go, now!" Luke exclaimed. "We berets will cover you!"

As Mrs. Hoffmann ran there, a vibration from behind the campus was heard, and out of nowhere, a helicopter came into view.

"Give yourself up, or die," the pilot said, just as the other helicopter came between them.

Everyone's heart pounded.

Their hands shook.

No one could think.

The Hoffmann boys had risked so much to get their parents free, but now, they were trapped between two helicopters and two machine guns.

"Drop all of your weapons," the pilot of the other helicopter said.

Patrick looked at his brother, his mother, and the rest of the group, and a mist came over his eyes.

What could they do?

Patrick looked over the strange assembly of people again.

Twelve tough green berets, a Corpsman, a bush craft enthusiast, some young woman, the niece of the leader of a secretive organization, and a gentle, frail, motherly woman, and himself.

Now apparently captured by the very evil that each one of them had been fighting their entire lives, whether knowingly or not.

He and his brothers exchanged glances. All thinking the same thing; *If we fight back, we'll die. If we give ourselves up, we'll probably die. But you never know, God's kept us alive this long. He can save us even now.*

Lord, save us, please, somehow, Angelica prayed.

She swallowed, tried to calm her breathing, and ignore her throbbing ankle.

"I'm willing die to defeat these boys in blue helmets," General Connor muttered, as if talking to himself. "I've protected this country, corrupt as it is, for more than a decade. But now, there's a tremor in my voice. Have I done enough?

Fight. Fight. Fight. That's all I've ever done. Lord, forgive me for forgetting you. "

The helicopter in front of them lowered in the college park. The other landed on the roof.

As the clock ticked on, sweat dripped down George's forehead. He looked at his older brother.

His eyebrows were dropped a little, as if thinking deeply and methodically.

Patrick laid his rifle down.

Find Out More in My Next Book . . . .

Sneak Peek into the Next Book

—————

A SCENE AND PORTION of, "Weather Warfare".

Patrick rubbed his hands and stomped his feet in an effort to get warm. He glanced over his shoulder at his family and Tabetha and Angelica. He breathed out, and you could see his breath.

His sisters, Elizabeth, Martha, and Susan huddled underneath a wool blanket and they had on many layers, but they still shivered.

The door of the abandoned shepherd's shack rattled against a strong gust of wind, and the door suddenly blew open.

The Hoffmann family and the girls awoke in surprise, and Patrick and Samuel hastened to secure it shut.

They could hardly hear each other over the roar of the wind as they looked for their tool box.

"Wheest!" Mrs. Hoffmann exclaimed.

"What's that vibration sound?"

The two older boys stopped their work and listened carefully.

The few small things they had on the beaten down mantle began to rattle. They all looked at it in shock.

They were all thinking the same thing. *Earthquake? Oh boy!*

"Earthquake posture, now!" Patrick and Samuel exclaimed, dropping to the floor.

They all threw off their blankets and went into the posture. They could hear many things rattling and they heard a lighting strike and thunder in the snow.

All of sudden, it quieted down. The wind, the thunder snow, and the earthquake tremors.

The Hoffmann family breathed again and raised their heads. They gave each other looks, and their eyes registered confusion.

Sarah sighed and got up stiffly. She went to the hearth and fumbled around clumsily for the coffee pot handle, using a blanket as a potholder.

As she poured the thin stuff, her hands shook and she spilt a great deal.

"Sarah!" Tabetha exclaimed angrily. "Look at how much you've wasted!"

Sarah closed her eyes at her own stupidity.

"You know we can't afford to waste any," Patrick said tiredly, and resumed his stomping.

———

"I'M HUNGRY!" BENJAMIN exclaimed, looking at his parents. Sarah sighed and went to a corner where there where stacks of wooden crates. She brought out a packet of a meal, ready-to-eat, and dumped the not appetizing meal into a camping pot.

Benjamin looked on the proceedings with disgust. There was nothing else to eat except such things.

"You hear something?" Angelica asked, trying to rid herself of her British accent.

In the somewhat quiet, the nickers of the Hoffmann horses were loud and clear enough to hear.

"They got out!" Samuel raggedly exclaimed. George and Patrick followed after their brother as he shot out the door.

In the snowstorm, the brothers could hardly see a thing, the weather of Wisconsin being unforgiving at that moment. But George could make out a dark smudge of brown.

"There!" he screamed as he pointed, but his words were muffled by his thick scarf. He caught his brothers' attention. They moved toward the figure.

Before they could get to the animal, he was spooked by thunder and bolted. The stiff legs of the Hoffmann boys tried to get the horse back, but he was already long gone.

They tried to find the other horses, but the wind was getting more bitter and after being in the beat cold for more than ten minutes, they gave up and went inside.

"Did you get them?" Elizabeth asked before coughing.

Disappointed, the boys shook their heads and stood by the hearth.

"Well, what are we gonna do? We can't travel without our horses!" Martha cried, her golden waves shaking in her agitation.

Patrick sighed, remembering baked chicken, scalloped potatoes, and broccoli. "We'll stay here as long as we can, then move out when the weather permits. The horses couldn't have gone far. Maybe we'll search for them again when the snow lets up."

The door burst open.

A man in UN uniform leveled a pistol at Susan.

———————

"IT'S CERTAINLY NICE to get even, isn't it?" the man moved inside and three other UN officers came in and shut the door. "This is a nice sanctuary you have here."

The man removed his balaclava. Tabetha, Angelica, and Mr. Hoffmann gasped in disbelief. *Officer Igor!*

"Look who we have here! The three escaped prisoners. Ha! Well, all things worked out. I've recovered the three POWs and gained a couple more. How about that?"

The Hoffmanns looked at each other. *All things work out...just not for him and his buddies.*

"You're a very sneaky bunch, you know that? You've managed to evade my men for months," Igor settled down by the hearth, and the other officers took over watching the Hoffmanns. They began to handcuff the Hoffmann family and the two girls.

Patrick hardly took notice of the officers roughly handcuffing him. "Escape and evade."

Igor scowled at him. "You know your friends, those annoying Roberts? My men tell me they've finally destroyed them."

The Hoffmanns gasped loudly. The Roberts owned a large piece of land in Montana with other families. The Hoffmanns and Roberts had met each other at a conference, and had immediately become fast friends. Mr. Hoffmann had invested much money in his friend's property, even though he did not live there.

"I never expected that places like this still exist," Igor said, looking around the room.

"You'd be surprised all that you don't expect," Samuel muttered angrily.

"No need to be so bitter. People like you will always die," Igor replied smugly.

"Likewise for you," Samuel shot back.

Igor decided to ignore him. "Can't very well bring you to a FEMA camp in this storm. When it lightens up we'll go."

Outside there was the sound of stomping feet, neighs, and the snarling of a mountain lion.

"What is that?" Igor jumped up. He snapped his fingers. "Enrich, Nicolas, you two go check," he instructed. They nodded and went outside.

There were sounds of screaming and gunshots. The only officer left besides Igor was trying to avoid the inevitable. "Uh, Officer Igor?"

"What is it, Sasha?" he asked, peeking out the window.

George was not properly bound yet, and looked for his handgun. Igor and Sasha both had their backs turned to him. He located his Glock and slowly backed to it.

"Well, sir, we don't have enough handcuffs for them," Sasha said, jabbing a thumb in George's direction.

Angelica noticed George's creeping, and almost feeling scared, she grabbed the gun and gave it George because she was closer.

He pulled it out of the holster and shot at the Igor and Sasha, who were being very unaware.

George gasped, not ever shooting anyone at such close proximity.

Quickly he handed the startled Angelica his gun and grabbed the hand-cuff keys from Sasha. Soon, his mother and Elizabeth were tending to the two shot men.

"Patrick, go outside. We need to know what happened out there!" Sarah said.

He nodded and with Samuel went carefully outside with their rifles. They were surprised to see a dead cougar and two dead mutilated men. There were sounds of neighing near the lean-to that the boys had built, and they walked carefully near there.

"The horses came back!" Samuel said, slowing his pace as to not spook the horses.

The boys were overcome with gratefulness as they tied the horses very securely to a post and secured their blankets on them.

Feeling numbed with cold, the two brothers went back inside. "The horses are back!" Patrick exclaimed when they re-entered.

Hardly anyone payed them any mind because they were trying to help Elizabeth, who had transformed into EMT mode.

"Get me a knife. Thanks. Hot water. Stroke the fire, Benjamin. Susan? Spread out two bedrolls. George, help me lift these two over there. On one. Three, two, one, lift! Okay, now this one..." "Give me the whiskey!"

"Drink this!" Elizabeth instructed the two men. "You need to be healthy and strong for your interrogation," she added.

At this, Igor muttered, "People will come looking for us." Elizabeth looked thoughtful for a minute. She got up and went to her older brother Samuel. "Sam, he has a point. Leave them and let's exfiltrate. In fact,"-she peeked out the window- "the snow seems to have quieted down enough, anyhow."

Samuel nodded in agreement and talked with Patrick.

"We're gonna leave this place," Patrick told the others, "Pack your stuff, put on more warm clothes. You have fifteen minutes," so saying, he began packing his own things. "Sam, George, saddle the horses please."

They nodded and put on their gloves to brave the extreme cold.

"You can't..." Sasha gritted his teeth against the pain. The bullet had gone through his lung, causing severe bleeding that none of them cared to stop. "You can't leave!"

"Don't get any crazy ideas!" Angelica brandished George's gun. Everyone looked at her in shock. She had been frightened of firearms when they had first met her.

Susan gave a small shake of her head and turned back to filling water bottles with hot water.

Benjamin and Daniel were folding blankets and rolling up sleeping bags.

Outside, the brothers had gone near the lean-to and had removed a tarp over a wide spider-hole they had dug for storing their horse gear.

They shivered as they tightened the horses' girths. The boys wandered back inside.

Samuel stopped in his tracks. George gave him a puzzled look. "Do you hear something?"

George blinked and his eyebrows shot up. He stood in the cold for a few moments. "No. Why?"

Before Samuel could reply, a Russian Su-34 fighter jet was seen distantly in the snowy air. The brothers' jaws drooped.

"The spider hole, George!" Samuel cried, running back the way they had come.

The bounded quickly under the spider hole and covered their heads.

"BOOM!"

Inside, the others stopped what they were doing and froze.

"BOOM!"

Patrick peeked out the window and saw flames. "Get in the cellar!" he exclaimed.

The others lifted the metal door of the underground storm cellar and jumped down. As soon as they were down, Patrick and Mr. Hoffmann rushed to get all their packs and other supplies down before the shack collapsed.

"BOOM!"

Susan screamed. Patrick and Mr. Hoffmann jumped down and closed the door just in time.

"BOOM!"

They covered their heads.

"George and Samuel!" Mrs. Hoffmann exclaimed. "They're still up there!"

THE BROTHERS LOOKED in horror as the shack with the others went up in a puff of flame and smoke, taking some of the ground with it.

Oh, God. Help them! was all George could pray. His older brother looked just as distraught.

The Su-34 continued to randomly bomb parts of the forest, but soon, it flew away. In the light snow, the brothers lifted the roof of the spider-hole off and climbed out anxiously.

As they edged nearer, their steps slowed, reluctant to get too close. Their common sense overcome their fear and they looked for skeletons. Upon finding none, they looked farther away from the shack.

The brothers turned around when they heard rattling. Their eyes then focused on the entrance to the storm cellar.

With relieved grins, George and Samuel looked at each other and hastily went to the cellar door.

Samuel cleared the debris of the top with his rifle, and George grabbed the handle.

"No, George!" Samuel warned, but it was too late.

"YELP!" George let go of the handle quickly and rubbed it in the snow.

Samuel rolled his eyes and looked around for a strong stick.

"Hey," he called George, "Big dummy! Get that stick," Samuel pointed.

George nodded sighed and went to fetch it.

Using the stick, the brothers were able to open the cellar door.

"Guys?" they called down. They listened carefully. They heard a cough and soon saw Tabetha's signature Titian hair.

"Beth!" Samuel exclaimed in surprise. "Are the others down there?" She nodded and sat in the snow, still coughing. Soon everyone was up out of the cellar, and George and Samuel were grateful when they saw what Patrick and Mr. Hoffmann had managed to get before the bombs.

Samuel slumped down beside his mother and opened his canteen. "You thirsty, Mother?"

"No thank you, son."

Samuel gave her a side-eye look.

He got up and helped Patrick fill up their large saddlebags. "Do you think it was *their* friends?"

"Well, who else could have sent them after us? I'm sure that they had a back up plan if things didn't 'work out'. I am *so* sick of dealing with these guys. Can't we just have some relief?"

Samuel sighed. "When you're worthy, the worthless hate you, brother. You know that already. I do, too. We're Marines! But we're also Christians. That makes us double worse to the UN. Life's not fun."

"I guess we could be doing something worse," Patrick said.

"Like what?!"

"Algebra."

"Dude! I'd rather be doing algebra than this. Anything's better than being shot at or bombed!"

Patrick chuckled, but Samuel shook his head.

Tabetha came over and helped fill up the saddlebags.

"How are they doing, Ms. Lee?" Patrick asked.

She hesitated. "Nobody's saying a word. Just...sort of...too tired to care anymore. What's a bomb now? It'd be like...washing the dishes. It seems like a completely normal thing,"- she clicked her tongue and shook her head- "So sad."

They were surprised to hear crunching of twigs behind them.

They heard a shriek from Daniel. The brothers and Tabetha looked at each other. "Stay here!" Samuel said. Tabetha swallowed as the two Hoffmann boys darted away. She felt someone creeping towards her and turned around. She gasped. She was face-to-face with

a Chippewa brave. The brave also looked surprise to see her, a "female warrior". The brave held a bow.

The brave lowered his bow but Tabetha felt edgy. "We come in peace," the brave raised his hand. Tabetha lowered her rifle and raised her hand as well, knowing that it was an old Indian custom to see if the person had five fingers.

———

SAMUEL AND PATRICK ran quickly back to the shack area. They did a double take when he saw numerous Indian braves in buckskins and with bows.

The brothers looked at each other.

They were shocked to see the Indian braves lower their bows. The leader raised his hands in peace.

Mr. Hoffmann turned around. "Patrick, Samuel, Tabetha?! Indians are here! They come in peace!"

The brothers sneaked out of their hiding place.

"What's going on here?" Patrick wondered.

"We are part of the Chippewa band in this region. We have seen the smoke from here, as well as heard the explosion. We have known you have been here for many days. We could no longer keep our curiosity away. I am Medweganoonind, chief of my band. Named after one of our great chiefs of long ago."

"Med-wega-noo-nind?" Daniel asked.

"Why are you here, in our woods?" the Chief asked, as Tabetha and the brave came in view.

Mr. Hoffmann calculated his answer to the very primitive man. "We seek refuge from...bad white men. They seek to harm us, but we have been falsely accused. It was they that captured us for no reason at all. Naturally, my children wanted justice for me."

"These men, they are called peacekeepers?"

"Yes."

"But in reality, they are *war makers*?"

"Yes, everything you have said is true."

"We will take you to our camp. We have also fought the ones who make war. They are like the bear. At first, gentle and kind. But when the bear grows up, aggressive and dangerous."

Susan tried not to snicker at such a description.

"Thank you.......Med... Sorry."

"Chief is fine." The chief signaled to move out, and the Hoffmanns hastened to saddle up.

The Hoffmanns and their newly found Indian friends traveled many miles to their bands' camp.

Spread out, in a clearing next to a river and mountain, there were many wigwams and fires. The Hoffmanns were very surprised.

"You seem to know much more about Indians than other people we have crossed paths with," the Chief suddenly said to Patrick.

Patrick chuckled as he got off his horse. "Well, that's only because we like watching Western TV shows and movies."

The chief nodded. "I see."

He led the Hoffmanns and the girls to a wigwam in the center of the camp. He entered the warm place. A woman stirring something in a pot over the fire turned her head at their entrance. There were also two little boys and one girl in the wigwam.

The chief went to them while the Hoffmanns took in their surroundings. "This is my wife, and two sons and a daughter."

"Please, make yourself at home."

"We thank you for this, Chief," Mr. Hoffmann said. "How can we repay you?"

"Together, we can be great leaders among our people. You, among the whites, and me among the Chippewa. Now, with things coming to a great collapse, you and I can help rebuild the society. Together we can change the world! With hard work, determination, and the will to survive and press on, we can achieve anything.

CAPTIVES OF CHICAGO: THE QUEST TO ESCAPE

The sky's the limit. It's a new age, with new possibilities! We can do any-thing in this time!

Special Gift

GOD HAS A GIFT FOR You! The Plan of Salvation:

There is no formal prayer of salvation as many churches would have you believe, God's Word is very clear - there is only one way to get to the Father in heaven and that is through Jesus Christ (John 14:6). Jesus says that you must be born again to enter into heaven (John 3:3-5).

Salvation is simply the first step in building an open and honest relationship with God. We all have sinned and fallen short, but there is Hope in Jesus Christ - Just cry out to God in sincerity and honesty asking for forgiveness and for Him to Save you, sanctify you, and fill you with His Holy Spirit - Ask for His will to be done in your life on earth as it is in Heaven and That's it, now just keep it real with God.

A Warning:

The Christian walk is not an easy life on the surface. The Word of God says that we will be hated in all the world for Christ namesake (Matt. 24:9). The Bible says that in the last days are enemy prevail against us physically until Christ returns to save us (Dan 7:21, 22). Furthermore, we must endure hardship as a good soldier of Jesus Christ (2 Tim 2:3) and yet we are never alone in this, God promises us that He will never leave us nor forsake us if we believe in him (Matt.28:20).

In everything we go through we have the peace and joy of God which surpasses all understanding (Philp. 4:6-8) The Bible declares, "For I consider the sufferings of this present time are not worthy to be compared with the glory which shall be revealed in us". (Rom 8:18). However, in all these things we are more than conquerors through Jesus Christ (Rom. 8:37)

Stay in Contact

STAY IN CONTACT WITH the American Christian Defense Alliance, Inc. through Our Website At: ACDAInc.Org

Join Our Mailing List

We also Greatly Appreciate You Signing Up for our Mailing List and Providing a Good Rating and review for this Book. Your reviews help other people like yourself find this book and benefit from its contents.

If You or Your Family have been Blessed by this book please let us know by dropping us a line through our website at acdainc.org

Find All Our Books Online

———

SOME OF OUR BOOKS:

Salvation for Your Unsaved Mom: 10 Things to Tell Your Mom Before She Dies

Embracing Pregnancy, Your Child, and Parenting: A Christian Parenting Guide to Offer Encouragement During the Wonders, Joy, and Hope of Your First Child

Parenting: How To Be A Great Parent And Raise Awesome Kids

Parenting Special Needs Children: A Christian Guide to Parenting Children with ADHD, Autism, Asperger's, and other Psychological, Behavioral, or Physiological Disorders

Kids and Prayer: Pray with Your Kids and Teach Them How to Pray

A Vague Notion: How To Overcome Limiting Beliefs of Fear and Anxiety Through the Word of God

Prayer: Your No. 1 Prayer Book To Learn To Be A Strong Christian Prayer Warrior That Prays With Powerful Prayers In The War Room To Overcome And

Defeat The Enemy

Race Relations in America: A Christian Guide to Unite Christians in the Faith

Martial Arts Ministry: How To Start A Martial Arts Ministry

Biblical Bug Out: Don't Bug In - Follow The Calling

CAPTIVES OF CHICAGO: THE QUEST TO ESCAPE

Christian Prepping 101: How To Start Prepping

How to Finance Your Full-Time RV Dream

Make Money: A Beginners Guide to Start an Online Business, Work from Home, Make Money, and Develop Financial Freedom

Additional Formats

———

THANK YOU FOR READING this book. Your support and the support of others continue to humble us and enable our Ministry to grow. We hope and pray that this book has blessed you in some way. If you enjoyed this book, consider purchasing it as a gift for someone who could benefit from it.

We Greatly Appreciate Your Support as Well as You Sharing this information, including links to our books with Others on Your Social Media Platforms

Thank You Once Again for Your Support; We Know God Will Bless You as You Have Blessed This Ministry

Thank You Once Again for Reading

I hope that you have enjoyed the, "Sneak Peek" into my next book, "Weather Warfare". Lord willing I will be releasing it before December 25th

May God Protect You and Your Family in these Last Days.

———————

LAUREN MCKENZIE